SOME THINGS PEOPLE SAID ABOUT THE FIZZLEBERT STUMP BOOKS

Wonderfully told, fabulously eccentric, and certain to leave everyone in the family wearing a broad smile.

— Jeremy Strong

Fantastically funny

— Primary Teacher

Walks a high-wire of daft ideas and deft storytelling, ringmastered by a narrator who intrudes on the action with hilariously incongruous asides. Top fun at the Big Top.

— Financial Times

One of the funniest books I've ever read!

— Amy, 10, Girl Talk

If you like funny, exciting and entertaining books, read about Fizzlebert Stump. The author keeps the reader gripped by the way he ends each chapter, making you want to read on to find out what happens next. Even my mum enjoyed this book and I had to keep telling her what was happening!

— Freya Hudson, 10, Lovereading4kids

FIZZLEBERT STUMP

THE BOY WHO DID

in his

FIZZLEBERT STUMP

THE BOY WHO DID

P.E.

in his

PANTS

A.F. HARROLD

ILLUSTRATED BY
SARAH HORNE

BLOOMSBURY

LONDON OXFORD NEW YORK NEW DELHI SYDNEY

Bloomsbury Publishing, London, Oxford, New York, New Delhi and Sydney

First published in Great Britain in February 2016 by Bloomsbury Publishing Plc
50 Bedford Square, London WC1B 3DP

www.bloomsbury.com

ISBN 978 1 4088 5339 9

Typeset by Newgen Knowledge Works (P) Ltd., Chennai, India
Printed and bound in Great Britain by CPI Group (UK) Ltd, Croydon CR0 4YY

1 3 5 7 9 10 8 6 4 2

For Simon Dunn

CHAPTER ZERO

In which the hero is introduced and
in which a predicament is outlined

Once upon a time there was a princess and there was a shoemaker and there was a puppy called Simon and there was an angry washerwoman with curlers in her hair and not one of them had anything to do with this book, so you can stop reading about them now. In fact I don't even know how they got in the first sentence. I turned my back for one

minute and there they were, knocking on the page like an unruly mob of characters with nothing better to do but cause trouble in the first paragraph of someone else's story. Ignore them. Ignore them all. Except the puppy, who's been well behaved, all things considered. If he keeps quiet while I get on with the rest of the book, I might let him make a surprise appearance in Chapter Seven. He's cute, don't you think? Lovely ears.

So, as I was saying before I started writing, there's a boy. He's about *this* tall and has hair that looks like *this* and has a pair of eyes on the front of his head the exact same colour as *this*. His name is Fizzlebert Stump, which shouldn't come as a surprise to anyone since it's on the front cover, and he lives in the circus. (Not *the* circus, to be accurate, just

a circus, although it's the one he calls home, which makes it quite *the* in his mind.)

His dad's a strongman and his mum's a clown. One of them has a little waxed moustache and lifts enormous weights up above their head and the other has a red nose and pours

custard down their trousers. I'll leave it to you to decide which is which.

So, where was I? There's a boy called Fizzlebert, or Fizz for short, and he's lost in the forest and it's late at night—

What?

I hadn't got that far?

Sorry, I got distracted thinking about the little puppy Simon, and his big eyes, and do you know what? I don't even like dogs. I prefer cats. (Some cats and dogs get on fine, of course, but usually they don't. *Proverbially* speaking, cats and dogs fight like sheep and wolves. And that said, what are wolves, if not just big, angry dogs? (Sheep, on the other hand, have nothing in common with cats, except that they both get excited by the sight of a ball of wool: the cat wants to play with it;

the sheep wants to see if it was someone she knew.) But that's enough of that.)

Here's where we've got to with the story: Fizzlebert is in the woods, it's late at night, it's dark, he's on his own and he's lost.

OK, that's the introduction done. I'm going to have a break now, look in the dictionary for some more words and get back to you in a minute with an explanation of how he came to be where he has come to be in the way in which he is there. Clear? Super.

CHAPTER ONE

In which a boy has a wee and
in which a clown drives off

A travelling circus is the best sort of circus there is, because when you open the curtains of your caravan in the morning there's always a new view. (Admittedly, the new view looks pretty much the same as the old view, because the circus always parks up in the town park and parks are usually flattish green places with a few trees and a duck pond, but if you like green, trees, ponds and ducks, then why start complaining now?)

It was while the circus was travelling from one place to another that Fizz ended up in the predicament I mentioned earlier and which I'm trying (if you'd stop interrupting and asking questions) to tell you about.

It was late at night. Fizz was asleep in his bed. He'd done the straps up tight and put his earplugs in and was dozing snorily, but happily, dreaming of things I can't tell you about because I don't know what they were. He'd done the straps up because the circus was moving to a new pitch and he was trying to sleep. It was safest to strap in when you went to bed, just in case there were any sharp corners or sudden stops. As the old saying

had it, 'Better safe than bruised in a heap on the floor.'

Fizz had woken up in the dark and noticed immediately that the caravan wasn't moving. He couldn't hear the hum of the engine of his mum's car either. He took his earplugs out and still couldn't hear it. They'd stopped.

Fizz unbuckled, got out of bed and snuck a peak through the curtains. He wondered if they'd reached their destination or if they'd just stopped *en route* (which is a French phrase meaning 'on route' but said with an accent (don't look at me weird, I don't know why people use it either, but they do)). There were trees, certainly, but he couldn't see a duck pond or the big flat open green grass of a park. He would've asked his mum or dad, but they were in the car that pulled the caravan and he wasn't.

No problem. He just pulled his dressing gown on over his pyjamas, slipped his slippers on his feet, opened the front door, climbed down the steps and looked around.

They'd pulled over at the side of a road that sliced straight through a thick dark forest. It was summer still, but the night air was cool. Somewhere an owl hooted and the slow wind rattled high branches.

Inside the car his mum and dad were arguing over a map. He could see the light of a torch waving around and a giant piece of paper being folded and unfolded.

I already told you that Fizz's mum, Mrs Stump or The Fumbling Gloriosus (to give her her proper clown name), was a clown, but

what I didn't say was that she was responsible for driving the clown car between shows.

A clown car is smaller than a normal-sized car. In fact, it looks to be slightly smaller than a clown and part of the joke of a clown car is that the tallest clown in the circus climbs out of it, picks it up, puts it in under his or her arm and walks off. Fizz's mum wasn't the tallest clown, and fitted in fine, but his dad, remember, was the strongman, rippling with muscles and sporting a neat black waxed moustache. Although the moustache didn't take up an awful lot of room, his muscles were squeezed into the car in such a way that, had he been heavily tattooed, half the windows would have looked like television screens showing programmes about tattoos.

(A clown car only has a small engine and

is soon left behind by the rest of the circus, which is why they were still driving in the middle of the night, while everyone else had already arrived in their new park.)

Fizz tapped on the car window. Startled, his dad let out a high terrified wobbly yelp of a scream and leapt in his seat (or vice versa). His head burst out the top of the car, sending the sunroof flying through the air.

'Oh, Fizz!' he said, when he'd got his breath back. 'You didn't half give me a fright.'

Fizz's mum climbed out of the car and, carrying the steering wheel, walked over to where the sunroof had landed, picked it up, tucked it under her arm and turned to face Fizz.

'Fizz,' she said, 'you shouldn't be up at this time of night. You get back in the caravan.

Once your dad has agreed which way up the map goes we'll be off again. We wouldn't want to leave you behind, would we?'

'Goodness, no!' his dad agreed. 'That would be like the start of an adventure in one of those books you read. We don't want that, do we?'

'No,' Fizz said, joining in, 'I really wouldn't want to be stuck in these dark and forbidding woods all by myself, would I? That really would be like the opening scene of a bad novel.'

They all had a little laugh at this.

Once they'd stopped laughing Fizz's mum said, 'Well, Fizz, go on. Back to bed.'

She made a motion with the sunroof to suggest movement and Fizz headed back towards the caravan.

Before he got there he had a sudden feeling.

He stopped walking and looked around.

His mum had pushed his dad's head back inside the car and had clipped the sunroof back in place. She was about to climb back in when she noticed that Fizz had stopped moving.

'What is it, darling?' she asked.

'I need a pee,' he said.

Inside the caravan was a little chemical toilet, shut away in a tiny toilet cubicle about the size of a very large shoebox. It smelt of lingering blue chemicals and despite everyone's efforts to keep it clean and tidy, it still wasn't anyone's favourite room in the world. It's one of the problems of living in a caravan, always moving around, this problem of plumbing. It was the one thing Fizz was jealous of when he read about people who lived in houses that didn't move. They used a toilet, pulled the chain and everything was swept away, down pipes and along sewers and off to who-knew-where. But in a caravan you carried it all around with you until you got a chance to empty it out. Until then, everything you'd *toileted* sloshed around somewhere underneath you.

'Well, get in the caravan and go,' his mum said.

'I'm going to go behind a tree,' Fizz said.

'Oh, OK,' his mum said. 'Don't go far.'

'No, I'll just go over here,' Fizz said, pointing into the darkness by the side of the caravan.

'Then straight back in,' his mum said.

'Of course,' he said.

'OK,' she said.

Fizz nipped into the dark, said 'Hello' to a tree, had a pee and was about to walk back over to the caravan when a gust of wind rose up from nowhere, ran along the road, caught itself up on the caravan door and slammed it shut.

His mum and dad must have been listening out for such a noise, since as soon as it slammed, the car coughed into life, belched a cloud of exhaust fumes into the glow of the red lights at the back and slowly began to haul the caravan away.

'Hey, stop!' Fizz shouted, running after them, but they didn't hear, and the last thing he saw was the caravan vanishing round a corner at the bottom of the hill and then the forest was in darkness.

Fizz watched the lights of his parents' car and caravan vanish with a sinking feeling in the pit of his stomach (it started higher up, but settled there). He wasn't afraid though, because he was sure they'd notice he was missing any minute now and turn the car round.

Any minute now.

He waited.

Any minute now ...

After a while he sat down on a hump by the side of the road and waited some more.

He looked at the place on his wrist where a watch would've been had he been wearing a watch, which he wasn't.

Out of the dark between the trees Fizz could hear scritchings and scratchings and cricks and cracks as things moved about.

An owl hooted from far off. Mice scuttled for cover. And as he listened more closely, other noises wandered into his ears. Things he had no picture to go with: noises that could have been the snuffling of wolves or the creaking of a gate or the splash of a frog in a pond. In the dark it was hard to know what was what.

The moon tiptoed out from behind a cloud, making the road look silvery and the darkness slightly less dark.

Fizz looked at his wrist again. In the moonlight he could just make out the time. It was a hair after freckle o'clock, but he didn't feel very sleepy.

Looking up at the strip of sky that ran between the two stands of trees he could make out stars, here and there, speckled

on the blackness. And he noticed how the blackness of the sky wasn't absolute, wasn't as dark as he first thought, because the trees, the edges of the woods, were blacker still. The pitch-black silhouettes of the treetops hid the stars from view, and set the road-shaped strip of the sky into a dusty velvet grey contrast.

Enough of that beautiful descriptive writing, Fizz thought. His parents hadn't come back and he was an idiot to just hang around in the middle of a road through the middle of a forest in the middle of the night. He got up and started walking, heading in the direction the car had gone. It seemed the most sensible thing to do, and Fizz was nothing if not an occasionally most sensible boy. This way when his parents turned around and came

back for him they wouldn't have so far to drive, which, knowing his mum's car, could only be a good thing.

It was harder walking in the dark than he'd thought. He tried walking on the soft verge at the edge of the road, but he kept tripping over hummocks or hillocks or holes. (If you want to get an idea of how it was for Fizz, go out in the garden and try walking in the flowerbeds with your eyes shut.) Why walk, you might ask, on the bumpy grassy forest-edge, when there's a perfectly smooth road to be had? That's easily explained: Fizz's dressing gown was a dark blue and he knew better than to walk in the road in the dark wearing dark clothes. That's a sure recipe for getting knocked over. However, brushing acorns and beetles out of his hair, he gave in and began walking on the tarmac, but he kept an especially wide ear open for cars coming up from behind (and eyes open for headlights up ahead).

And it was lucky he did, because not five minutes into his midnight hike he heard a distant rumble. It was hard to say if it was behind him or in front of him until he turned and saw the glow of headlights lighting the sky up at the head of the hill he was walking down.

He watched the wavering beams shining on the sparse wisps of cloud high overhead, and then the lights crested the hill: two headlights and, higher up, other lights on the top of a lorry's cab.

Besides the noise of the truck, there was another sound, though he couldn't pick it out, not on its own, not to say what it was. Was it a rattle, perhaps? A scratching?

One of Fizz's hobbies was reading books. In an earlier book I wrote about him, he visited a library and got so overexcited by the sight of so many books that he accidentally had an adventure (see *Fizzlebert Stump: The Boy Who Ran Away From the Circus (and joined the library)* (Bloomsbury, 2012)). The sort of books he most liked were adventure stories in outer space or with dinosaurs or robots or ghosts (he had yet to find one about the ghost of a robot dinosaur haunting a space station, but he was hopeful).

Something he *had* once read, in a book of ghost stories, was about hitch-hiking, which is where a person stands at the side of the road and sticks out their thumb. A nice person in a car sees the person's thumb, knows they want a lift, stops the car, asks them where they're

going, says that they're going near there and gives the hitch-hiker a lift.

For a moment Fizzlebert stood on the verge with his thumb up, hoping the truck driver would see him and maybe give him a lift further up the road to where his parents were still trundling onwards, but then the thought jumped up in his mind, waving its arms, letting off flares and shouting in his face that the truck *wasn't slowing down.*

And, what was more, it hogged the whole width of this narrow country road. Trees on both sides were hitting the cab, making that scratching rattling sound, and Fizz realised that even where he stood, on the verge, would be in the lorry's path.

As the dazzling rack of lights hurtled towards him he did the only thing he could,

which was to take another step backwards, into the woods, out of the way.

At the last moment it seemed the driver caught sight of Fizz, because there was a long deep hoot of a horn, and the screeching squeal of brakes. The lorry hurtled forward, hardly slowing down at all, while the smell of burning rubber wafted through the woods.

(When no crunch of a collision came, the driver, supposing that he hadn't seen a boy after all, knowing that he certainly hadn't *hit* one, lifted his foot from the brake pedal, and continued on his way. Night driving, he knew from long experience, was a tiring job and at about two in the morning you sometimes saw things out of the corner of your eye which weren't really there. Maybe he'd caught the glimpse of a startled deer, or maybe it had just been nothing.)

Soon the red glow of the truck's rear lights and the rumbling noise of its engine had gone and the forest was empty of the music of manmade machinery again. Only nature's night-time noises filled the place: the calls of frogs, the creak of trees in the breeze, those owls calling again and the scurrying of mice and voles in the undergrowth, the footsteps of foxes, etc.

But where was Fizz?

He'd taken a step back and had found his foot treading on empty space, like when you walk downstairs in the middle of the night and miscount the steps and, expecting the floor, you find there's further to go and your heart leaps and your stomach flips and fortunately

you've only misjudged by a few inches and everything's all right and nothing's broken. Fizz, on the other foot, had misjudged a lot further than that.

He had stepped into empty air and then gone (as gravity dictates) downwards. The rest of him followed and he tumbled down a steep slope which rolled away from the road.

Having a circus upbringing is good for some things. For instance, it meant Fizz didn't go to school. Instead he took his lessons with the various members of the circus's ensemble. So, for example, the circus's new escapologist Epistrophe Locke took him for metalwork (Locke wasn't an enthusiastic teacher and, when the idea had first been mooted (which means mentioned) he had

tried to get out of having to give the lessons, but had failed).

More pertinently, the Twitchery Sisters, *Mary and Maureen The Human Trampolines* (the circus's leading acrobats), taught Fizz geography, but neither Fizz nor the Twitchery Sisters much cared for geography, so instead, sometimes, occasionally, not very often really (if anyone asked), they'd show him how to do backflips and somersaults. Fizz wasn't brilliant at them, and often fell over halfway through, which meant that instead of learning how to jump, he actually learnt how to fall.

So, as Fizz fell down the slope, in the dark, he tucked his head in and wrapped his arms round himself and he rolled like a hedgehog through ferns and brambles and over dead

logs and bracken until finally he came to a stop.

He unrolled himself and, having no broken bones, stood up. From what he could piece together he'd fallen quite a long way through the dark. Now, in the middle of the forest, the darkness was total. It was black, black, black everywhere he looked.

He turned around.

Black, black, black.

He turned around again.

Black, black, etc.

Not a glimpse of light.

He looked up and, perhaps, he really wasn't sure, saw the twinkle of a white pin-prick star through the blackness of the trees. But then it wasn't there, so maybe he hadn't seen it at all.

He turned round again, and realised that, with all this turning, he no longer knew which direction he'd fallen from. He didn't know where the road was. And if he didn't know where the road was, then he didn't know which way home was, because his mum and dad were on that road and they *were* his home.

Fizz, a boy not easily given to worry, was given to worry right then, done up nice with a bow and glossy black wrapping paper.

Well, here we are, the end of Chapter One and Fizz is finally, as promised, properly Lost in The Woods. Maybe Chapter Two will shed a little light on his predicament.

CHAPTER TWO

In which it is very dark and in which a dream is dreamt by a dreamer

I can't stress just how black the night was in the middle of the woods, with the moon lost above the treetops and the nearest town over a mile away, the road missing and the circus unguessably distant. It was really black. Black. You could write the word 'black' on a sheet of paper in really bold capital letters, fold it up, swallow it, hide in a trunk

in a cupboard in a ship's cabin so cheap it's below the waterline (and thus porthole-less) with all the lights turned out, and only then would you get an idea of how black the darkness was.

In the darkness Fizz stumbled, tripped and flustered his way through ferns and brambles and branches. He tore his pyjamas and muddied his slippers. He got twigs in his hair and was poked in the eye. Eventually he gave up the 'walking around' as a bad plan.

He had been trying to follow the ground uphill, thinking that that way he'd find the road, but it hadn't worked. It was so uneven and so hard going that he couldn't work out which way the wood sloped.

He sat down with his back to a tree and felt low. He was lost, scratched, dirty and tired.

There was nothing he could do until morning. Once the sun had come up he'd be able to find the slope he'd fallen down, find his way back to the road, and then, maybe, by following it ... well, *maybe*, it would lead somewhere *circussy*.

But as he sat there, breathing quietly, listening to the night, he found he could see a little of his surroundings for the first time. His eyes were growing better in the dim light, much better than they had been in the thick dark. There were ferns growing all around and there in front of him, cutting through underneath them, was what looked like a path. It certainly wasn't a path *he'd* made, because he could see that over on his left, broken down and trampled. This path passed under the plants, was only a foot or so high, but was so clearly made by *something* that curiosity got the better of him.

He leant down close and could just make out, in a patch of mud softer than the surrounding earth, a little paw print. It was an animal's track, and the tunnel through the ferns must be, he realised (since he wasn't stupid), an animal's path. He ran through what it could be. What lived in woods like these?

As he pondered the question, a twig snapped.

Nearby?

It sounded like it was nearby, but it was hard to say. Fizz sat still. He held his breath. (Not in his hands, but in his lungs, which is the best and most normal way to do it.) And then, out of the darkness, down the ferny tunnel waddled a shape he recognised.

It was a badger.

In certain books badgers are wise old codgers, with spectacles and walking sticks and slippers and cosy homes under the roots of trees. They're a bit curmudgeonly, but once you've got through their gruff exterior layers they're actually friendly and always eager to help an animal in trouble, especially one lost in the woods on a snowy night (it was late summer in this book though, so no snow tonight). That's what Fizz was thinking. And of course, in that sort of book, the badger would stop and look up at Fizz when it *almost* bumped into him (some authors consider it amusing to take the mickey out of short-sighted people), then grump to itself before saying, 'Well, well, well. What have we got here?'

And Fizz would say, 'Please, sir, I'm just a boy, lost in the woods.'

And the Badger (spelt with a capital 'B' now, just to let you know that's his name, as if there's only one badger in the world) would say, 'Dear me, a human child, in the woods at this time of night? Botherations and ditheringtons. What shall be done?'

And Fizz would say, 'Please, sir, might you help me find my way out again? My parents will be mighty worried, I'm sure.'

And the Badger would look Fizz up and down, growing dewy-eyed and say, 'His parents are worried. Oh, the poor child! Oh, the poor parents, out there waiting, not knowing what's become of him! Why of course I'll help you, you poor childerkind of the two-legs.'

And the Badger would stomp off into the undergrowth and say, 'Follow me, keep up, come on!'

And Fizz would scurry along as quick as he could, listening to the Badger's footsteps just in front of him until they reached a round front door in amongst the roots of a great old oak tree and the Badger would pull a key from his waistcoat pocket and unlock the door and say, 'Come in, come in.'

And Fizz would say, 'But this isn't where my parents are, is it?'

And the Badger would say, 'Of course not, but while I put the kettle on why don't you use the telephone to ring them? Let them know you're OK.'

And Fizz would think about the great spreading tree above their heads, amongst

whose roots they were nestled, and say, 'Actually, I think I'll let them know I'm *oak-y*,' as if he were the clown Unnecessary Sid.

And the Badger wouldn't see the joke, and would fuss to himself at the kettle, rummaging in old cans looking for a pair of unused tea bags.

And Fizz would lift the telephone from its cradle and dial his mum's number and listen to the phone ring and ring, and eventually he'd get her answering service and he'd leave her a message, telling her he was taking tea with the Badger and she shouldn't worry, he'd probably be home in the morning.

And the Badger would pour out two steaming cups and bring them over to the little table before the fireplace and Fizz would sit in a big armchair and sip his hot tea,

which would be weak, but delicious. And the Badger would lay a little plate of sandwiches on the table and stretch and yawn and shake himself.

And Fizz would notice how big Badger's teeth were, how sharp, and would lift up one of the sandwiches and take a bite.

And the Badger would turn the key in the front door so that it locked with a click. And he'd drop the key into his waistcoat pocket and pat it as if to make sure it were safe and snug and secure. And the Badger would chuckle a nasty little chuckle which he'd turn into a cough and say, 'Oh, my chest. The winter air does get to it so. Oh yes, my little boysicle.'

And Fizz would wonder exactly what it was that was in the sandwich he was eating, and

he'd say to the Badger, 'Dear sir, Badger-my-chum, what is it you eat? I thought it might be roots or acorns or something like that, but I just can't tell.' And then his teeth would find something hard and he'd pull a button from his mouth, a button that had been in the sandwich.

And the Badger would say, 'What do I eat, it wants to know? Oh sir, oh little human, oh little bald pinkly friend of mine, Fizzlebert-my-lad what I eat is ...' and the Badger would turn and the firelight would flicker in his eyes, red as blood, as his voice dropped low, '... is children!'

And Fizz would see the thick sharp yellow-white teeth glint and his fairy tale would be over.

But thank goodness this isn't *that* sort

of book. I allow no talking animals in these books, because there are no talking animals in the world (except for parrots who learn swear words from the old ladies they live with and dogs that can say 'Sausages' unconvincingly).

In the real world the badger (with a lower case 'b') just looked up at Fizz, puzzled for a moment about what he was, and waddled off into the night, forgetting the sight of the sleeping boy almost immediately.

Fizz, on the other hand, woke from his dream with a yell. His heart was beating fast and he gulped quick lungfuls of the dark forest air.

That had been a nightmare and no mistake.

The feeling it left was so bitter that he resolved not to sleep any more. He didn't want to fall back into the badger hole. Looking at his

wrist he could just make out that it was still a hair past freckle o'clock, but a different freckle now. The sun would be coming up in just a few hours. He could stay awake that long and then he could make a start on finding the road.

But before he could do anything there was a crashing in the ferns and a light was shining straight in his face.

'Aha! I knew I 'eard somefink,' said a voice. 'Put yer 'ands up where I can see 'em. You're my prisoner ... boy.'

Someone was pointing a torch at Fizz's face and he was so dazzled, especially after so long in the dark, that he couldn't make out who was behind the light, but he could tell, from the voice, that it was ... a girl.

And verily, Fizz was afraid.

CHAPTER THREE

In which a girl leads the way and
in which a boy does as he's told

Fizz put his hands up. He didn't know what else to do.

'Good,' the voice behind the torch said. 'Now, tell us what you're doin' 'ere in me woods, out at night like this. You a poacher, boy? You tryin' a steal you some pheasants or somefink?'

Fizz wasn't sure what a poacher was, but he'd had poached eggs before and they

were eggs boiled in water without their shells, unlike boiled eggs which are poached eggs with the shells left on. But he wasn't in hot water. Or was he? People said, 'Oh, you're in hot water now,' when you were in trouble, didn't they? And he was in trouble, wasn't he? So, maybe he *was* a poacher, but what had the girl said about pheasants? Was he stealing them? He knew what pheasants were because he'd seen an act at a different circus once called *Dorothy Crescent & Her Pleasant Pheasant*. As far as he could tell a pheasant was a bird with impeccable manners which always lifted a wingtip feather when drinking tea. It was a nice bird, but he wasn't planning on stealing one.

'I don't think so,' he said after some thought. 'I'm lost.'

'Lost, eh?'

'Yes, lost. You see I got left behind up on the road and then I fell down this hill and—'

'You 'ungry?'

'Um, no not really,' said Fizz.

'Well, follow me,' the voice said, somewhat confusingly.

The torch swung around, away from Fizz's face, and headed off through the ferns.

Not knowing what else to do, Fizz followed.

As he walked he caught glimpses of the girl silhouetted in the torchlight. She was about his age, he reckoned, and had short scruffy hair poking out from underneath a little beret or cap. Every now and then she'd stop and turn around and shine the light at a tricky bit of path.

She kept talking.

'You know, I 'eard you fall. *Crash bang wallop*, you went. I 'eard you from a mile away. Woke me up it did. Got me outta bed and int'rested. Then you went snappin' and bangin' through them woods and then it all went quiet for a bit but then I 'eard you snorin'. Well, I 'eard someone snorin' and there ain't usually no snorin' goin' on in them woods, so I reckon it was you, yeah?'

Fizz didn't say very much other than, 'Can you slow down, please?' because he was a bit embarrassed and because she was going quite fast.

After maybe ten minutes, the girl's torch shone upon the painted wooden wall of a little house.

''Ere we are then,' she said. ''Ome.'

Fizz had never lived in a house without wheels, but that didn't mean he didn't know one when he saw one. There was a light shining on the porch and he thought he could see a glow behind the curtains in the window.

The girl opened the front door and ushered him in.

Fizz was hopeful. Where there was a house there might be a telephone and where there was a telephone there was a way for him to get in touch with his mum and dad. He had their phone number written down on a piece of paper in the inside pocket of his coat just in case of exactly this sort of emergency.

(And in case he ever lost the bit of paper, he'd taken to carrying an old tuna sandwich in another pocket in order to attract Fish, the circus's sea lion, to his emergency location.)

But the hope he'd been filled with upon stepping into the house fizzled away in a puff of gloom when he realised that the piece of paper and the sandwich were inside his jacket, which was in the clothes cupboard to the left of the toilet back in the caravan. All he had in the pocket of his dressing gown, which was what he was busy wearing, was a little label that said, 'Wash at forty degrees'.

'Is that you, Piltdown?' called a voice from further in the house.

'Yeah, Gran,' shouted the girl, who, it seemed, was called Piltdown.

'D'you know what time it is?'

'Yeah, Gran.'

Now they were in the light Fizz could see his rescuer properly. She was a girl, probably around his own age, certainly around his own

height. She had scruffy red hair, cut short, and a big grin on her face as she held a finger to her mouth. She reminded him a bit of looking in a dirty mirror. It was rather uncanny. They could almost have been twins. If you didn't look *too* closely.

'Don't let 'er know you're 'ere,' she whispered. 'She don't like strangers much.'

'Where have you been, dear?' the grandmother shouted.

There was the sound of moving about in the other room, as if an old lady was getting out of bed.

'Poachers,' the girl, Piltdown, shouted, while opening a door and pushing Fizz forward. 'In there, 'n' be quiet,' she whispered.

'Poachers?' Piltdown's gran said, coming into the hallway.

'Yeah, I thought I 'eard someone out there, scuttling around. Just went to 'ave a look, 'n' get a bitta fresh air too.'

'Hmm. Find anyone?'

'Nah, either they'd gorn, or they weren't there to begin with.'

As Fizz listened to the conversation he felt around himself (it was dark again). To his side were tall wooden things which might have been mops and to the other side were flaky cardboard boxes on shelves. As he edged his foot carefully forward, so he could lean more comfortably against the shelves, something went SNAP and clung to his slippers.

'What was that?' he heard the old lady say.

'What was what?' Piltdown answered.

'I thought I heard something?'

'I told you, it's poachers. I 'eard 'em earlier.'

'Hmm.'

Fizz wanted to reach down and dislodge whatever it was that had snapped shut on his slipper. He assumed it was a mousetrap, and was glad his toes hadn't been right up at the edge. He'd got these slippers for Christmas

and had been told, 'You'll grow into them'. He was getting there, slowly.

Piltdown's gran had obviously shuffled out of the hallway because the cupboard door opened a sliver and Piltdown's voice whispered in.

'Boy,' it said. 'You'd best come out now. She's in the kitchen. We'll 'ide you in me bedroom 'til she's gone out to work. No bother. Quick, run now while she's busy.'

She pointed across the hall to a half-open door.

Fizz did as he was told, because there didn't seem anything else to do.

Secretly he would have liked to have spoken to her gran, because she might have been able to find a way to get in touch with his parents, because that's what grown-ups did.

She'd have more of an idea than her granddaughter would, probably. But at the same time, he'd had a bad experience with an old woman before, and the way Piltdown was so insistent about him not meeting her made him a little bit afraid of her, without even having seen her.

'I'm goin' back to bed,' Piltdown shouted at the kitchen from her bedroom. 'Just for a coupla hours.'

'OK, dear,' her gran shouted back. 'Just make sure you're up for school. I already had a letter from them. You know *I'm* the one that gets in trouble. You will go, won't you, dear?'

''Course I will, Gran,' Piltdown shouted. 'Dontcha trust me or somefink?'

'All right then. Night, Piltie dear.'

'Night, Gran.'

Piltdown shut the door.

Fizz was stood in the middle of the room, slightly dazed. Several thoughts were going through his head at the same time. Firstly, he was thinking he'd never met two people who shouted so much. Secondly, he was amazed because Piltdown had a bedroom all to herself, that wasn't used as the kitchen-cum-living room during the day. Thirdly, he was worried about his parents. How would they be coping with him missing? He hoped they were all right. Fourthly, he was yawning. Fifthly, he thought Piltdown was a boy's name, but didn't say anything because whether Piltdown was a boy's name or not, Fizzlebert was still a silly name. Sixthly … sixthly, he couldn't remember what he was thinking. He was too tired, hence the aforementioned yawning.

Piltdown noticed.

'Oh crikey,' she said, whispering again. 'You look dead on yer feet, boy. Look, you get into bed, get a few hours' kip before morning.'

'But ...' said Fizz, tiredly.

'No buts,' she answered firmly. 'I'll keep guard. Ain't nuffink to worry about.'

Half reluctantly, Fizz climbed on to the bed, pulled the sheet up over him, dressing gown and all, and lay his head on the slightly smelly pillow.

'I can't keep callin' you Boy, Boy,' Piltdown said, switching off the light. 'What are you called?'

'Fizzle*mumble*,' murmured Fizz, almost asleep already.

The next thing Fizz knew there was daylight in his eyes and the bed was bouncing up and down like a dreadfully unhappy ship in the middle of a surprisingly sunny storm.

Morning had broken.

And I'm breaking the chapter there too. That's quite enough adventure for one night. What will the morning bring? Oh, mystery and romance, perhaps? Who knows. Who knows? *I* know.

CHAPTER FOUR

In which breakfast is burnt and
in which our hero moves on

'Stop bouncing, please,' Fizz said with a yawn to the girl who was bouncing on his bed.

'Get up then,' she said, jumping off the bed and running out of the room.

Fizzlebert reached down to undo the straps and buckles but, of course, there weren't any.

He swung his legs over the edge and said,

'Where have you gone. Piltdown?'

'I'm in the kitchen,' she shouted.

Fizz crossed the room and gingerly stuck his head round the bedroom door (gingerly in both senses, being at this moment both a red-headed young man and a cautious, careful one).

'Is your gran around?' he whispered.

'Nah,' Piltdown shouted back. 'She's off at work in the forest, choppin' trees.'

'Oh?' Fizz said.

''Ow d'ya like yer toast?' Piltdown yelled from the kitchen, a trickle of black smoke following her words through the door.

'Well done?' Fizz said, cautiously.

He followed the smell of burning into the kitchen.

The clock on the wall said eight o'clock. That

was way earlier than he usually got up. At the circus there are a lot of late nights. There's no going to bed until the show's over and the audience has all left, and then there's tidying up and taking off make-up (if you're a clown) or singing lullabies to your horses (if you're a horse trainer), and sometimes the Ringmaster gets everyone together to tell them how brilliant they were, or not, depending on how the show's gone and how much his indigestion is playing up.

Fizz stifled a yawn.

There was a plate with a couple of glistening black squares on it.

'I buttered 'em,' Piltdown said.

'Thanks,' said Fizz.

Seeing the toast made him think of his mum, and his heart sank. He was still lost. They must be going mad with worry. They'd

be out looking for him. He ought to find his way back through the woods to the road. That would be the sensible thing to do. (The reason the toast reminded him of Mrs Stump, his mother, was because she'd recently started making toast for the family (instead of the more normal candyfloss and cornflakes or popcorn and popcorn). If you've read some of the previous books about Fizz you might remember her predilection for rhyming sandwiches: ham and jam, cheese and peas, pork and fork (this last one had to be eaten carefully). So she had invented a breakfast of her own: toast and ghost. Some people got cheese on their toast, some got jam, some Marmite. Fizz had to try to eat his toast while Mrs Stump draped a white sheet over Mr Stump and

made him go, '*Wooo-oo-oooo!*' Whether that was more annoying than toast burnt to a crisp was a matter of debate, but remembering it made Fizz pause.)

'I've got to go,' he said, after nibbling the corner of one black slab.

'Already? But you only just got 'ere,' Piltdown said, sitting opposite him at the kitchen table.

'My mum and dad will be worried,' he said.

Piltdown took a big bite of her slice of toast and, after a second's thought, spat it out on to the plate.

She scrunched her face up.

'I don't like toast,' she said, and changed the subject. 'What was you doin' in the woods last night?'

Fizz explained about living in the circus

and about getting left behind and falling down the slope and getting lost and then getting found and after that he didn't need to explain any more because she'd been there for the rest. (You know all that stuff, so I won't bore you with his exact words, but if you've got a friend nearby maybe you could pretend to be Fizz and let them be Piltdown and you can see how *you* would tell the story. Then when you've done that swap over and do it again. Then when you're satisfied, read on.)

'So you ain't from round 'ere?' Piltdown said.

'No.'

'And no one round 'ere knows you?' she asked.

'No.'

'Ain't it funny,' she added. 'You've got the same hair as me.'

'Yeah,' said Fizz, 'funny.'

She was right, they did both have the red hair in the same not-quite-a-haircut.

'Interesting,' she said, a thoughtful look on her face.

'What?' asked Fizz.

'Look at yourself,' she said, changing the subject again.

She pointed at the sleeves of his dressing gown and at the bottoms of his pyjama bottoms. They were muddy, dirty, torn and tatty.

'Tell you what,' she said. 'I'll lend you some clean clobber. I mean you can't go wanderin' around all day in yer PJs, can you? That's weird.'

She went off to her bedroom and Fizz could hear rummaging.

'Here you go,' she shouted.

He went through and found she'd laid out a pair of black trousers and a shirt and jumper.

Fizz got dressed (he always wore clean underwear under his pyjamas in case of a midnight caravan emergency, so luckily he didn't have to borrow her knickers). It all fit, though he had a little trouble doing up the buttons on the shirt (they were the wrong way round to what he was used to).

He looked at himself in the mirror.

'Piltdown?' he called.

She came back in.

'Piltdown,' he repeated. 'Is this a *school uniform*?'

It was. The jumper had a badge on it that he couldn't read in the mirror.

'Yeah. It's me spare one,' she said. 'Don't worry about it.'

She was wearing a pair of tatty jeans and had a jacket pulled on over her T-shirt.

She was holding a battered leather satchel.

'Look,' she said, 'I've made you a packed lunch for yer journey.'

She handed him the bag and he looked inside.

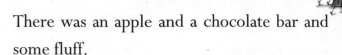

There was an apple and a chocolate bar and some fluff.

'Thank you,' he said. 'Mmm, fluff, my favourite.'

'Good,' she said, apparently not noticing his joke, or at least being too polite to mention it. 'You wanna get back to the 'igh road through the woods, yeah?'

She walked him out the front door, on to the little wooden veranda.

'Please,' he said. He hadn't thought of any better plan than going and waiting where they'd left him.

'Well, don't go back through there.' She pointed over her shoulder at the looming forest. 'Nah, you'd just get lost. I know a quicker, easier way. Go down there.' She pointed at the dirt track that lead off from the cabin, a rutted mud road just wide enough for a car. 'After a coupla hundred metres you'll hit a road, turn right and that'll take you to another road, turn right again and that's the road through the woods. Bingo.'

'Thanks,' said Fizz.

'Go on,' she said, pointing up the track.

Fizz pulled his dressing gown on over the top of his jumper and tucked the pyjamas he'd been clutching into the satchel.

'Keep it,' Piltdown said. 'Keep it all, and good luck to ya.'

Fizz walked off, his slippers flip flopping on the dry mud.

After twenty metres he turned around, expecting to wave at the girl who'd saved him but she'd already vanished. The cottage was still there though, looking lived in, so he

was pretty certain she hadn't been a kindly ghost or some weird dream. Which, on the whole, he was pleased about.

And there goes Fizz, trudging down the track on his way back to the place his parents lost him. They're bound to be there, aren't they? Don't you think? Wouldn't your parents have spent the night waiting by the roadside for you to just wander back?

Hmm.

Is this the best plan Fizz has had? Do you think it's going to work out well? (I'll give you a hint: have a look and see how many pages there are left in the book you're holding. If there are only a couple then Fizz probably finds his mum and dad in the next chapter and everything's fine. If it looks like you're only about a quarter of the way through, then maybe something else happens before Fizz finds his way home. What do you think? (Answers on a postcard to Pointless Fizzlebert Stump Non-Competition, Bloomsbury Publishing, 50 Bedford Square, London, WC1B 3DP, UK. The best answer gets no prize, as do all the answers. But it'll be a nice way for me to prove to my publishers that someone actually reads these books.))

CHAPTER FIVE

In which a man stands beside a
car and in which a name is read
from the top of a satchel

'Ah, there you are, at last,' said the man who was standing by the car at the end of the track. He was tapping his watch and sighing extravagantly. 'I was about to come in there and get you,' he added.

Fizz looked behind him to see who the man was talking to.

There was no one there.

'Come on, come on,' the man said, pointing towards the car.

He had a scraggly thin beard and wore a rough dark green suit. The elbows of his suit jacket had leather patches on.

'Me?' Fizz said, pointing at himself.

The man sighed and ran a hand through his shaggy hair.

'Yes, of course you. We'll be late if you don't get a move on.'

Fizz was really quite confused by this.

If the man had been someone he knew then he'd have been much happier. If he was someone Fizz knew that would mean he was someone from the circus and *that* would mean he'd been found. But this man was a stranger and Fizz knew better than to start getting into

strangers' cars without asking a whole lot of questions first (and even after the questions he probably still wouldn't get in, because a stranger questioned is still a stranger).

'I think you've got the wrong person,' Fizz said, wondering if he ought to go back to Piltdown's cottage.

'Look, just stop being silly. Come on, Piltdown.'

'Piltdown?' Fizz said.

It wasn't all that embarrassing to have been mistaken for the girl. After all, he *was* wearing her spare school uniform. At least there'd been a simple explanation. This stranger wasn't one of those strangers to be wary of, he was just a man who was mistaken.

The man held the car door open and said, 'Get in. I haven't got time for this.'

'No,' said Fizz with a smile. 'You see there's been a funny mistake here. You think I'm Piltdown, but I'm not. She's back at the cottage. Shall I go get her?'

The man sighed deeply, shook his head wearily and rubbed the bridge of his nose.

'Give me strength,' he said. 'We don't have time for this. Just get in the car.'

Before Fizz had the chance to realise something was wrong and make a run for it, the man grabbed him by the satchel strap.

'Look, little madam,' he said, leaning down so their faces were close together, 'I've got a job to do. I'm paid to get you to that school. No one cares how I do it, not any more, not after the run around you've given us all last week. I'll stick you in the boot if needs be, but you're going to get in that car, right now.'

His breath smelt of acid drops.

'But,' pleaded Fizz, feeling desperate, 'I'm *really* not Piltdown. My name is Fizzlebert Stump and I live in the circus and I got lost in the forest last night and Piltdown found me and made me breakfast, but really I'm just trying to get home to my mum and dad.'

The man listened to Fizz gabbling and then shook his head and said, 'No.' Firmly.

He pointed down at the top of the satchel that was hanging in between them. In the big black letters of a permanent marker it said: *Piltdown Truffle's Bag — Now Buzz Off And Leave Me Alone.*

He pushed Fizz towards the car's open door.

'Get in,' he said.

Fizz didn't know what else to do. He could try running, but he didn't think he'd get far. He could try reasoning with the man, but it didn't seem the man was open to reason. He could try shouting, in case the real Piltdown Truffle heard and came running to his rescue (again), but he had the feeling in the pit of his stomach that he had been, as they say in

the circus business, stitched up like a kipper. (Not that there's much call for kipper stitching these days, not since they invented edible glue (but still, a saying is a saying and who are we to start making changes now?).)

Maybe when he got to the school he'd be able to talk to someone more sensible. Maybe there'd even be a telephone there he could ring his mum from (if he miraculously found his coat, which was in the caravan, with the phone number in). OK then, if not *phone* her, maybe he'd find some sensible helpful grown-up who'd listen and help him get home.

The door slammed and the man climbed in the other side.

'Look, Piltdown,' he said as he put the key in the ignition. He seemed a bit calmer. 'I know it can be a bit daunting starting a new

school, but you'll make friends in no time at all and it's a good place. You'll enjoy it, really, as long as you stop being a stupid, horrible, rebellious little madam.'

The car pulled away and under the noise of the engine the two of them sat in an uneasy silence. Eventually Fizz broke it.

'Who are you?' he asked, in order for me to stop writing 'the man' every time I talk about him, which is getting a bit annoying.

'What do you mean?' the man said (see what I mean?). 'We've met before. Last Friday? *And* last Thursday? You don't remember? How about last Tuesday?'

'Um, no? Sorry,' said Fizz.

As the man drove he slipped a small rectangle of card out of his jacket pocket and handed it to Fizz.

'You hear of any other kids bunking off, you just give me a ring on that number,' he said, pointing at the card. 'We could be friends, me and you, you know.'

Fizz read the card. It said: *T. Mann — Independent Truant Officer — for waifs and strays and runaways — all ages retrieved, minimum of fuss, maximum results.* There was a series of letters and logos and a phone number.

'What's the 'T' stand for?'

'Mind your own business.'

Fizz very nearly said, 'That's a funny thing for a 'T' to stand for,' but he thought better of it.

After a drive of just a few minutes the car pulled up in a car park in front of a low white building with lots of windows.

A short woman with a face like a friendly otter's and a colourful blazer jacket with big lapels and a glittery brooch in the shape of a crocodile wandered over to the car. Fizz noticed such details because he'd seen an otter in a previous book, there was a crocodile in his circus, and he was generally able to tell men and women apart (which was more than some people in this book so far, he thought).

'Ah, Mr Mann,' she said, leaning down (though not very far, already being a short person) and looking through the window at Fizz, 'I see you've brought our recalcitrant ne'er-do-well back into the fold. Splendid.'

'Yes, here she is, Mrs Scrapie,' Mr Mann said, unclicking Fizz's seatbelt. 'And if you need me later on, you have my number.'

'I hope that won't be necessary.'

'Of course.'

Mrs Scrapie opened Fizz's door and, because he couldn't think what else to do, he got out, still clutching Piltdown's satchel. He was sure there was no point pointing out Mr Mann's mistake while Mr Mann was still there.

'Cheerio,' said Mrs Scrapie as she slammed the car door.

She stood with a hand on Fizz's shoulder and they watched as Mr Mann drove off.

'Now,' the woman said when they were finally alone, 'let's get you to class.'

'About that,' Fizz began, lifting up a finger.

'Piltdown Truffle,' Mrs Scrapie said, sharply but kindly, in a way that clearly meant, 'Shush'.

Fizz was hurried through a set of doors and down a corridor and round a corner and through some more doors, round another corner and down one last corridor, up to a final door. All the time he tried to explain that he wasn't who she thought he was, but she never let him get far enough into his explanation for it to make sense before she cut him off with a curt, 'Now, now,' or a smart, 'Hurry up,' or a dismissive, 'I'm not listening, la la la.'

This wasn't going brilliantly and Fizz worried about his parents worrying about him. He wished there was a way he could get in touch with them, but he couldn't think how.

His only option was to wait, be patient, be alert, watch out for a chance to either

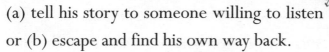

(a) tell his story to someone willing to listen or (b) escape and find his own way back.

At least, he thought, he was only in a school. It wasn't as if he had been kidnapped by bank robbers or aliens or angry wasps. How bad could school be?

Although he had never actually been in one before, Fizz had read about them in some of the books he'd picked up from the various libraries they passed by in the circus. (In case you're wondering, some of the libraries gave him self-addressed envelopes to post the books back in, some let him return the books to libraries where the books hadn't come from, and some of them insisted he only borrow unpopular books that no one would miss if he didn't bring them back for a year or two. It depended on which Local

Authority the library in question belonged to.) So, having read a bit about schools (they weren't his favourite sorts of books since often they didn't have *any* robots in, let alone aliens), he knew there'd be a tuck shop somewhere round here where he could get some chocolate when he felt peckish and all the kids would have funny nicknames for each other like Fatso or Big Ears or Jonson Minor. He knew they were always having sporting competitions against other schools and he'd have to get a scarf in the school colours. And sometimes they had owls.

Mrs Scrapie pushed him into the classroom and said, 'Mr Carvery, look who it is. Young Ms Truffle has deigned to return.'

Fizz looked around the room. There were no owls.

There was, however, a bald man in a tracksuit and thirty-odd kids in school uniforms staring at him. (Not, let's be clear, thirty *odd* kids. I just mean there were *about* thirty (say, more than twenty-seven but fewer than a hundred-and-thirteen, if I had to guess) normal, run-of-the-mill, common-or-garden kids, grey and boring and probably without any special powers, hidden skills or fire eaters for friends.)

'Excellent,' the man (who Fizz *assumed* was a teacher) said, running his fingers through invisible hair. 'Just what we needed.'

With that Mrs Scrapie shut the door and went off to wherever she went and Fizz was left in the classroom.

He fiddled with his satchel strap and looked at his slippers.

As a circus performer (he had recently started doing a strongman double act with his dad, and before that had put his head nightly in a lion's mouth) he was used to being watched by lots of people. Here he was being looked at by only thirty or so, and he found it awkward. When you were in the circus ring, doing your act, the lights were on you and you were concentrating and you weren't able to see the crowds. They were off in the dark and all you really knew of them was the hush as you did something daring and the roar of applause or laughter as you did something amazing. This was very different indeed.

He glanced up nervously.

No one looked like they were waiting for a brilliant act to start. In fact, they didn't look like they were about to have fun at all.

'Well?' said Mr Carvery, tapping his watch. (There was a lot of watch-tapping action going on this morning, Fizz thought.) 'Come on.' (And a lot of people in an awful hurry, he added.)

'What should I do?' Fizz asked in a quiet voice.

'Go sit down, Truffle,' Mr Carvery said, as if explaining something obvious to someone very stupid.

The other kids were sat in chairs around half a dozen tables. Fizz noticed a couple of empty seats, but none of them had neighbours who looked inviting. If anything, he got the impression he wasn't much desired at any of the tables.

'Where should I sit?' Fizz asked.

'Go sit next to Charlotte,' Mr Carvery snapped. 'And hurry it up. We've not got all day.'

This didn't help.

I don't know if you've ever tried looking round a room of kids and tried to spot which one is Charlotte, but it's not as easy as it sounds. Especially if you don't know who Charlotte is.

Fizz edged towards the nearest table with both an empty chair *and* a girl.

'No!' bellowed Mr Carvery. 'Take your coat off first, Truffle.'

'I don't have a coat,' Fizz said, feeling somewhat smaller than normal.

'Don't answer back. Have you no manners, girl? That *thing* you're wearing. Take it off and hang it up.'

'It's my dressing gown,' said Fizz.

There were a few titters from the back of the room.

Fizz draped the dressing gown over the back of the chair that seemed to be his. (The girl in the chair next door (Charlotte, presumably, since no one had said, 'That's not Charlotte, dummy') edged as far away from Fizz as she could physically get. If she still had a whole buttock on her chair Fizz would be surprised. She also slid her pencil case and workbook right over to the edge of the table as well.)

'No!' shouted Mr Carvery, tugging at his non-existent hair. 'Hang it up!'

Fizz looked around and saw a row of coats on one wall.

'Oh,' he said. 'I see.'

Despite all the shouting and staring and tittering he was trying his hardest not to let it get to him too much. He was a circus star, he wasn't easily daunted. He was Fizzlebert

Stump, he thought. Or possibly Piltdown Truffle, his mind whispered, and then he wondered where the girl had run off to. She'd seemed so nice, to begin with, and now this.

Fizz pushed some coats aside and found a peg. He hung his dressing gown up and walked back to his table.

'Very well,' Mr Carvery said, brushing non-existent locks of hair out of his face. 'Maybe now, if you don't mind, we can begin?'

'Yes,' Fizz said. 'Go ahead.'

There were some laughs from behind Fizz which Mr Carvery hushed with a blazing red-eyed stare.

Technically it *had* been a question that he had asked Fizz, and Fizz had answered it extremely politely, but apparently, it turned out, this hadn't been what the man

in the tracksuit expected, wanted, desired or liked. Fizz had done wrong. (I only mentioned the tracksuit again there because I think it's important to remember that this is a grown man, who is, let us remember, at work, who is wearing such a horrible, casual, unpleasant set of clothes. It's Monday morning at this point in the story, so they're clean and fresh, but he was the sort of man who wore the same tracksuit right through to the end of the week, because 'it's practical'. You didn't want to be close to him on a Friday afternoon. And it wasn't even as if he did a lot of sport. Like most teachers, he watched from the sidelines, blowing his whistle, riding his golf cart and hurling incoherent encouragement at the players, although whenever one of the lady teachers happened

by he would hop out and start running on the spot and doing stretches, but fortunately they remained unimpressed.)

'Not another word from you,' he snarled at Fizz, before talking to the room in general. 'OK, class. Get out your workbooks and pencils. I want one page of news. "What I did at the weekend." You've got twenty minutes, then we'll read some out. Let's get going.' He clapped his hands to encourage action.

Next to Fizz the girl, presumably Charlotte, unzipped her pencil case and pulled out a glittery blue pencil with a wobbly dragon on the end. She then produced an exercise book, seemingly from nowhere, clumped a hand down between her and Fizz, leant over and began writing. The other kids at the table did the same.

Fizz didn't have a book or a pencil. All he

 93

had in his satchel was an apple, a chocolate bar, some fluff and a set of tatty pyjamas. None of it sounded useful.

'Excuse me,' he whispered, nudging presumably-Charlotte. 'Can I borrow a pencil?'

'No,' she hissed. 'Not after last time.'

Fizz didn't know what he'd done last time, because he hadn't been there then. He guessed Piltdown hadn't been wholly respectful of presumably-Charlotte's property, and she'd not looked at him closely enough to know he wasn't her.

'I'm not her,' he whispered into the curtain of hair that, along with the defensive wall of her arm, separated the two of them.

'What?' hissed presumably-Charlotte.

'Piltdown. I'm not her,' he whispered. 'I'm an impostor.'

'Mr Carvery,' presumably-Charlotte said, raising her hand.

Mr Carvery looked up from his desk where he was sipping from a mug.

'What's she done now, Charlotte?'

'She's being weird, Mr Carvery, and she won't stop talking, and she's copying me.'

Mr Carvery sighed and made Fizz stand up and move to a table by himself that faced the wall in the corner.

He slammed down some rough paper and a short, chewed pencil and said, 'Just get on with it.'

And so Fizz, not knowing what else to do, no closer to finding his way home, did as he was told. He'd had a good weekend, so he had plenty to write, and maybe this would be his chance to tell the truth and to get it heard.

CHAPTER SIX

In which a teacher is upset and
in which a girl has hay fever

'The first thing that happened was I got up and I did that because Mum was already making breakfast and there were crumbs getting in my bed. Then she said, "Fizzlebert. This is the best toast in the world it's amazing toast," because she was making toast and boast for breakfast because she likes rhyming food. Then I went outside with my dad and we lifted things

up. Not straight away. First we did warming up by doing stretching, and *then* we lifted things up. He lifted a motorbike and a horse and I lifted a sea lion called Fish. He's my friend and he likes fish. Then we had lunch in the Mess Tent with Bongo Bongoton and Dr Surprise and it was meatballs in a sort of red flavour sauce with custard for afters. There's always lots of spare custard in the circus because—'

'Sit down!'

Fizz's hair riffled in the wind from Mr Carvery's mouth.

As he sat down he looked around the room.

Everyone was staring at him and a lot of them had their mouths hanging open.

Having just listened to John Jenkins talk about eating salad and to presumably-Charlotte talking about thinking about going to a museum the class had been electrified by Fizz's story, or so he thought.

'I won't have *lies* in my classroom,' Mr Carvery was shouting. 'What's important is what *actually happens*, all this made up stuff is useless. It fills your brains and dribbles out into the rest of your work. I won't be having it.'

He snatched Fizz's sheets of paper out of his hand and tore them up.

Fizz felt like picking the man up and holding him over his head, he was so angry. His muscles were rippling under the scratchy uniform, but he controlled himself. Doing something like that was a certain way to get into trouble. He had to be cool.

'What do you say?' Mr Carvery said.

'I don't know,' said Fizz.

'"Sorry",' said Mr Carvery, who was turning from red back to pink.

'Apology accepted,' said Fizz.

Oops.

He hadn't meant to say it. It just slipped out. As soon as it had gone past his lips he'd seen it and knew it was going to cause him trouble. If he'd had a magic lamp he would have rubbed it straight away, and taking those words back would have been his third wish

(after 'Seventeen more wishes' and 'A bigger caravan for Mum and Dad'), or maybe his fourth (after 'Please take me home' (although if he had had that wish he wouldn't need to take his words back, except perhaps for just being polite)).

Steam puffed from under Mr Carvery's tracksuit and, without thinking, Fizz rolled out of his seat and under the table.

In some of the school books he'd read teachers had canes or slippers or metre-long rulers and weren't afraid of whacking kids who misbehaved with them. And although Fizz's brain had a feeling that that didn't happen any more, his body had decided it wasn't taking any chances. It had rolled to safety without him even having to ask it. (It's this sort of split-second survival instinct that separates the kids who survive a circus upbringing from those who get squashed, eaten or custarded at an early age.)

The class was laughing now, little giggles and chuckles, growing into small guffaws and medium-sized snorks.

Fizz didn't know if they were laughing at him or at their teacher.

He watched Mr Carvery's legs turn away from the table he was under and the room fell silent.

Whoever they had been laughing at, they weren't laughing any more.

'Truffle,' the man's voice said, quietly and coldly, from above. 'You think you're so funny, don't you? Well, you can stay in at break time and write your news properly. No lies, no messing about, otherwise we'll have to call your grandmother in here and explain to her why you're in detention for *the rest of your life*.'

They listened to a few more kids.

Trevor Bacon had gone shopping with his mum and dad and they had bought some new underpants, and Romana Avalanche had listened to a CD about learning to play the violin on her headphones because her neighbours were violin intolerant.

From under his table Fizz found it oddly fascinating. He'd never spent much time listening to other kids, at least not ones without beards, and certainly not ones who didn't live in a circus. He felt like a bold adventurer paddling upriver to study some lost tribe deep in the jungle. He wondered if he ought to be taking notes.

After hearing about how Alfie Bacon (Trevor's younger brother (younger by three minutes, but Trevor never let him forget)) had also gone shopping with his mum and dad (and Trevor) and how he had also bought new underpants, a bell rang somewhere in the corridor.

Legs rushed past him on their way to break.

He crept out from under the table to find Mr Carvery handing him a new sheet of paper.

'Do it properly this time.'

Fizz sat down at the desk and wondered what he could write that would make the teacher happy. It was obvious the man wanted something normal and un-circussy, but Fizz found it difficult to think of what would be good. He could copy something one of the other kids had said, but Fizz hadn't ever been

shopping for new underpants, not as far as he could remember. (He was right. Five years ago the circus bought a brand new Big Top (it had been a successful summer and the Ringmaster was feeling flush) and his mum had paid Unnecessary Sid to sew Fizz lots of underpants out of the old material (which, when soaked for six weeks, was *almost* soft).

As he sat there tapping the pencil against his teeth Mr Carvery said, 'I'm popping out for a second. I have to talk to Mrs Wimple. Not a word from you two, OK?'

Fizz was confused. He counted himself: one. He hadn't thought there were two of him. He counted again: one.

Then someone sat down next to him.

He wondered who it was and quickly came up with the perfect plan to find out. He looked. (If only all plans, he thought, were as simple and as successful as this one.)

There was a girl sitting there with big brown hair, a little nose, two eyes, a mouth, eyebrows, a chin and a hearing aid in and behind one ear.

'Hello,' Fizz said, immediately breaking the one rule Mr Carvery had set.

'Hello,' said the girl.

She was already *much* friendlier than anyone else he'd met at school.

'I'm Dympna. Are you really from the circus?' she asked.

'Yes,' said Fizz. 'You believe me?'

'I do,' she said, simply. 'What's your name?'

'I'm Fizz,' Fizz said, holding his hand out to shake. 'Fizzlebert Stump.'

She laughed a sweet little giggle and shook his hand.

'You look like her,' she went on. 'A *bit* like her, but you're not her. She wasn't very nice. She put chewing gum on Mr Carvery's seat and she threw Charlotte's pencil case across the room and broke the leads in all her pencils and she kept shouting at me. I didn't like her.'

'Well, I'm not her,' Fizz said.

'I've got hay fever,' Dympna said, changing the subject, 'that's why I'm here.'

'At school? They send you to school for hay fever?'

'No, silly,' she giggled again. 'That's why I'm in at break. I'll start sneezing and sneezing and sneezing if I go outside. Mr Carvery lets me stay in and read.'

'I like books too,' said Fizz.

'Is that why *you* came to school?' Dympna asked. 'To read books? 'Cause I have to warn you, we don't do a lot of that.'

'No,' said Fizz. 'I was tricked.'

He tried to explain, as quickly as he could, what had happened to him and had just reached the point where he'd left Piltdown's house in the borrowed school uniform with

the satchel with his lunch in, when they heard footsteps in the corridor outside.

'Quick,' she said. 'Work!'

She pointed at his empty piece of paper and ran off to her own side of the classroom.

Just before the door opened she said, 'I know where the circus is.'

What?! Fizz thought.

The door shut with a loud click in the silence.

Mr Carvery's shadow darkened Fizz's desk and Fizz scribbled the beginning of a made-up sentence.

On Saturday we went shopping ...

Then the bell rang again.

Now, I know to you, who probably go to school most days, this might not seem like much of an adventure, but, without meaning to be rude, I have to say you're wrong.

For Fizz, this is *exactly* as much of an adventure as it would be if you were dropped in the middle of a circus and told to do an act. For Fizz this is a very weird situation. He's never had to sit up straight at a table or write about his weekend or listen to other children. He

feels a bit like a fish out of the frying pan and into the next lesson.

It's complicated.

It's sometimes (perhaps even always) important to remember that your *normal* is someone else's *weird*, and that someone else's *weird* is probably your *normal*, and vice versa. (That didn't quite come out right, but hopefully you get the gist. It's all about empathy, which means trying to understand by looking through someone else's eyes, but not in a literal drill-a-hole-in-the-back-of-their-head way (which is unkind, unpleasant and usually unnecessary), rather by using your imagination, if you see what I mean.)

Lesson six: Empathy.

CHAPTER SEVEN

In which a boy wears his
underwear and in which a puppy
makes a surprise appearance

Once the rest of the class rushed in after break and sat themselves down at their tables Mr Carvery began shouting again.

'All right, everyone,' was the first thing he shouted. 'In a minute you'll get changed into your P.E. kits, then we'll go out on the big field and you will do some organised running around.'

There were groans from the corners of the classroom but they went silent as Mr Carvery shouted some more, 'It's for your own good, boys and girls. Exercise is a treat. Now chop chop, get changed.'

Everyone bustled out of their chairs and rummaged in their bags and began changing into their shorts and T-shirts and trainers. The only things Fizz had in his bag were his pyjamas, and they were muddy and torn at the edges and he didn't think they'd be entirely suitable for this PE thing, whatever that was. (None of his teachers in the circus taught him PE, because in a circus you got enough of that by accident: there was always somewhere to run to, someone to jump over, something to lift up. So although the word 'P.E.' meant nothing to him, the words 'running around' and 'exercise' were enough of a clue for him to not embarrass himself by saying something stupid like, 'I'm sorry I need a new pencil first,' or 'William the Conqueror beat King Harold at the Battle of Hastings in 1066.')

Instead he embarrassed himself by saying, 'I've only got some pyjamas, but they're a bit tatty, sorry.'

To which Mr Carvery stormed and blustered, 'Well then, Truffle, it's a beautiful warm sunny day out there, you can do it in your vest and pants.'

The room went silent. This was getting interesting.

'Pardon?' said Fizz, who thought the man had just asked him to do exercise in his vest and pants.

'Vest and pants, now!' Mr Carvery bellowed.

Oh well, Fizz thought. Today started off weird, then it got weirder, but I need to talk to Dympna again. I'd best join in with the weird and not make trouble.

In a minute Fizz was stood in his underwear (and slippers). Fortunately they were relatively clean, even after the night's adventure, and didn't have embarrassing pictures of ponies or flowers on. In fact, odd as it seems, Fizz didn't feel embarrassed at all. He *almost* felt more at home than he had all morning.

As you might be aware, in between the last book I wrote about Fizz (*Fizzlebert Stump and the Girl Who Lifted Quite Heavy Things*) and this one (*Fizzlebert Stump: The Boy Who Did P.E. in His Pants*), Fizz and his father have been working hard to perfect their strongman (and son) act.

Mr Stump, in traditional strongman style, wears a little off-the-shoulder leopard-skin caveman affair, but for Fizz, who, being the smaller partner in the act, gets picked up a lot and twirled a little and who tumbles (in the sense of doing rolls and flips), something else is needed, something less *flappy*. So they made him what is effectively a set of sparkly vest and pants with glittery plimsolls.

So, you see, wearing his vest and pants wasn't the end of the world. In fact, it was a way for Fizz to feel momentarily more comfortable.

'Come on! Quickly! Out to the field, everyone,' shouted Mr Carvery, opening the outside door.

The kids rushed out, bouncing and hopping and giggling (a lot of them liked to do

anything other than sitting in a classroom learning, but they were the weird ones). Fizz dragged along behind them.

As he reached the door Dympna was waiting for him.

'I can't go out,' she said. 'I'll start sneezing.'

Fizz looked sad. He'd hoped he might get to talk to her again.

'But I made you this,' she said slipping him a folded-up piece of paper. 'It's a map. The circus is in the field behind my house. I saw them when I got up this morning.'

'Are you sure?'

'Great big tent? Lots of caravans and trucks and clowns and things?'

'That's it.'

'It's not far from here. Ten minutes' walk.'

 116

'Really?'

'Yeah, you're practically home, Fizzlebert Stump,' she said.

Her eyes were tearing up and her nose was beginning to run.

'Truffle,' yelled Mr Carvery, from outside the door. 'I just knew *you'd* still be here. Get out. And … What's this? You've made Dympna cry? You horrible girl. Get out now! Up to the field! I'll have you doing laps for an hour.'

Fizz, tucking the map into his pants, did as he was told.

'Thank you,' he said to Dympna as he left.

'Leave her alone, you horrible bully!' shouted Mr Carvery, slamming the door behind them and pushing Fizz in front of him up to the big field.

Dympna watched them go and went back to reading her book (which coincidentally enough was *Fizzlebert Stump: The Boy Who Ran Away From the Circus (and joined the library)* which had only just come out at this point in time and was another reason she'd suspected he wasn't Piltdown.

Mr Carvery was keeping his tracksuit from getting dirty or sweaty by driving alongside Fizz in a little golf cart.

Fizz was on his third lap of the school's big field. It wasn't actually all that big, Fizz thought, most of the parks the circus parked in were bigger than this, but still after two and a half laps he was growing pretty sick of it.

'Get those knees up, Truffle,' Mr Carvery shouted through a megaphone.

He was only two metres away from Fizz, so the megaphone wasn't strictly necessary, but at this point in the day Mr Carvery was being a P.E. teacher and P.E. teachers as a general rule aren't strictly necessary either, so it all balanced out.

In the middle of the field the rest of the class were playing rounders.

'Throw harder, Perkins,' Mr Carvery megaphoned at the boy who'd just thrown the ball.

He turned back to Fizz.

'Faster, Truffle, faster!'

Fizz was running at a sensible speed, not too fast because doing unlimited laps of a sports field wasn't a sprint. He was just going steady and because he was rather a fit young man, having helped out around the circus a lot, he wasn't even very out of breath yet.

This infuriated Mr Carvery who, wearing his P.E. teacher's metaphorical (and mega-phonical) hat, hated children who didn't struggle, whimper and collapse. (It was his job to give children 'encouragement'. He liked giving them 'encouragement', through his megaphone, and preferably in front of their friends. If he could give so much 'encouragement' that the wheezing embarrassed crying child wet itself as well, then his day felt complete. (What fun is there to be had encouraging a child who can actually already run or play cricket or table tennis well?))

As Fizz and Mr Carvery began their fourth lap of the field John Jenkins finally hit the ball with the rounders bat and sent it flying.

Fizz didn't notice until the ball hit the wire fence on his right and bounced across the grass in front of him.

'Well,' boomed Mr Carvery. 'Don't run past it, stupid girl. Throw it back.'

Fizz did as he was told, circled round, scooped up the ball in his hand and lobbed it back towards the middle of the field where the kids were roundering.

Unfortunately those kids didn't know that he was a strongboy, that is to say a junior strongman. His muscles were bigger and more excitable than a normal boy's and when he threw the ball he'd given it an extra boost without even thinking about it.

Thwack!

The ball drove straight through the middle of the kids, knocking them flying.

'Truffle!' yelled Mr Carvery. 'What have you done?!'

He veered his golf cart to the left and trundled at top speed towards the rounders game.

'Keep running,' he megaphoned over his shoulder. 'I've got my eye on you, you horrible little devil.'

Fizz kept jogging, while keeping an eye on what was going on in the middle of the field.

Mr Carvery had climbed down from his buggy, blown his whistle and was pulling children to their feet. Most of them were getting up by themselves, brushing themselves down and laughing. Only one of them, presumably Charlotte as it happened, was clutching her head. She was on her feet, but it looked like she might be crying.

'Sick bay!' Mr Carvery shouted through his megaphone to the poor girl, who was stood almost a whole metre away from him. (If she didn't already have a headache from being bashed in the bonce by a ballistic ball, then she certainly had one now.) 'Come with me!'

Fizz watched as Mr Carvery drove his golf buggy towards the school buildings. Presumably-Charlotte walked alongside, rubbing the side of her head.

'The rest of you, play rounders!' the teacher shouted. 'In silence. I don't want any complaints from the neighbours. I'll be back in one minute.'

Fizz took advantage of Mr Carvery's absence to stop running and pull Dympna's map out of his pants. It was warm and a bit wrinkled and as he unfolded it it flapped in the breeze.

Dympna had very neat handwriting and had labelled the map beautifully.

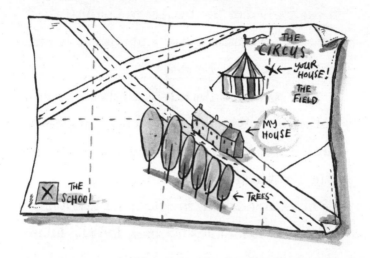

Here was the school and here was the field. And there was the road Fizz could see on the other side of the fence. And at the top it went round the field, and then there was another road, and another, and then a house marked 'My house' and behind that a big green patch she'd coloured in in felt tip with a picture of a tent in it and a sign saying 'Your house'.

This was going to be easy.

All Fizz had to do was go to the other end of the big field, jump the fence, run down three or four streets (ideally the ones on the map), and he'd be back at the circus. Even if his mum and dad, as he expected, were back in the forest looking for him, he'd be home and someone there would be able to get in touch with them and call them back. It was a foolproof plan. As easy as simple pie (which is the first pie bakers learn to make. It's pastry with a pastry filling: simple).

And I think it only right and fitting that as Fizz glories in the marvel of his having a perfect plan in front of him, we take a break between chapters and go off to have a cup of tea or a slice of pie, cheese, cake, cheesecake, mousse, soufflé, ice cream and/or sandwich, as you see fit.

(Oh, by the way, I didn't mention it at the time, because we were on the other side of the field, but in the street that runs along one side of the school field, an old man called Arbuthnot Crumplehorn was walking a small puppy called Simon, as promised.)

CHAPTER EIGHT

In which a boy runs away and in
which a grown man gives chase

Fizz looked at the fence, and he looked
back at the school building.

There were things about his time here
that he'd almost enjoyed (Dympna had been
nice, but most of it had been less than brilliant). Now it was time for him to take his
leave, he thought. He'd go back to where he
belonged.

128

He turned and, as inconspicuously as he could, in his vest and pants, jogged towards the back fence and the golden promise of home.

He didn't get far before he heard someone shout, 'Mr Carvery, Piltdown's running away,' and then there was a lot of whistle blowing followed by some rapid megaphonage ('Come back,' and the sort), but as far as Fizz could see when he glanced over his shoulder, no one was following him. (The teacher had only just come back out after dropping presumably-Charlotte at the sick bay. He was climbing back into his golf cart as he megaphoned, and doing two things at once was slowing him down.)

As Fizz reached the fence he leapt, caught hold of the interlocking diamond-shaped wire, and hauled himself up and over. All

 129

those lessons with the Twitchery Sisters and doing the occasional tumbling act with Fish had paid off.

He lowered himself down the other side and saw that the pursuit had begun.

Mr Carvery was finally zooming up the field in his buggy ('zooming' is perhaps the wrong word, since it suggests great speed: 'chugging up the field', 'trundling' maybe?).

Mrs Scrapie, the woman who had first met him when he arrived at the school, was standing by the school door. It looked like she was talking on a mobile phone while staring directly at Fizz. The round otteriness of her face wasn't as friendly as it had been when they'd first met – the eyes were narrowed. She wasn't happy.

Fizz turned his back on them and ran.

*   *   *

All these streets looked the same to Fizz.

He turned another corner, following the line on Dympna's map that linked the school and the circus. There were houses, side-by-side, two-by-two like unmoving square brick animals in a very flat ark filled with neat front gardens, pillar boxes and telegraph poles (so not very much like animals in the ark, after all).

Cats watched him as he ran past.

Dustbins stared at him with wide-open, freshly emptied mouths. (The dustcart turned the corner ahead of him and drove out of this book without doing anything important.)

Fizz stopped for a moment and leant against the pillar box to catch his breath and

 131

to have another look at the map, just to make sure he had it right in his head.

He looked back up the street the way he'd come and there was no one following him. Mr Carvery wouldn't have been able to get his golf cart over the fence; he'd've had to go back down the field and round. For the moment, Fizz was safe.

The map said if he went a bit further down this road, took the first turning on the left, then one to the right, he'd be at the entrance to the park. From there he'd be able to find his own way to the circus.

A postman whistled and Fizz started forwards again. He wasn't exactly running (to be honest, he had a bit of a stitch), but he wasn't walking either. It was something in between: ralking maybe? Or wunning? I don't know.

And it's not important because as he folded the map and as the postman whistled and as he began moving a car skidded round the corner ahead of him and revved its engine noisily.

Fizz recognised the car.

He'd ridden in it only that morning.

Mr Mann opened the door and pointed at Fizz with one hand. In the other hand he was holding something that looked like a bit of holey cloth (which will become important in a little bit, so try to remember).

'Piltdown Truffle,' he shouted down the street, 'I've come to get you. By the power invested in me by the Truant, Runaway and Incorrigible Scamps Act (2001, amended 2004) I am serving you notice that you're going back to that school, now!'

He began walking towards Fizz.

He was in between Fizz and the circus. Fizz couldn't go forward. He couldn't go back either: behind him was the school. So he looked around for another way out.

Aha! he thought.

There, to his left, was an alley that ran between two of the houses. It wasn't on his map, but if he went down it and then, when he got the chance, turned right, he was bound to reach the road he was meant to be on.

He ran.

Footsteps rattled behind him and he didn't turn to see whose feet they were because he knew full well it was the scruffy-bearded Mr Mann.

Fizz ran.

But not for long, because it turned out he had been mistaken.

This wasn't an alley, it was a passage that ran between two walls and then opened out into the garden behind the houses.

A young couple were having a picnic on the lawn (it was very nearly lunchtime) and Fizz apologised to them as he jumped over the picnic cloth and ran further into the garden (it was too late to turn back).

They stared after him, dumbstruck. It isn't often your picnic lunch is interrupted by a fleet-footed child in underpants, and it took them a moment to understand what had just happened.

'Was that?' said the young woman to her young man.

'I think?' he replied, not answering her question.

He lifted a sandwich to his mouth which was lucky because a moment later the rest of the picnic was crushed under the feet of a hurtling truant officer.

Mr Mann didn't apologise, he was too focused on the glimpse he'd had of 'Piltdown' up ahead, clambering over the garden fence. He wiped some cream off his glasses and kept on running.

He leapt at the fence and was pleased when it collapsed under his weight. He did a forward roll and bounced back up on his feet. That was easier than climbing, he would've thought if he'd spared the time to think, but he was far too busy for thinking; he was looking around for Piltdown Truffle.

Fizz had jumped at the fence, pulled himself

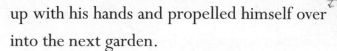

up with his hands and propelled himself over into the next garden.

He had expected to land on a lawn, or maybe in a bush, but to his surprise he found himself balancing on a clothes line. Fresh drying laundry dangled from the line under his slippered feet. He took one tightrope-step forward, wobbled and fell (tightrope walking not being one of the circus skills he had mastered).

After struggling through a variety of half-damp clothes Fizz landed on the ground and began running. He could see the garden gate at the side of the house. Through there and he'd be back on to the road, he thought, just as a tremendous crash smashed the air behind him.

He didn't waste time turning to see what it had been, because it was rather obvious. (And even if it wasn't what he assumed it was (a truant officer), it was still *something* that had just knocked a fence down behind him and that was probably worth running from too.)

So, he dashed across the patio and pulled at the bolt that kept the gate shut.

He yanked it open, slipped through and ran.

He wasn't running as fast as he had been before, he realised. Looking down he noticed that he was wearing a dress. Not wearing it very well, his arms weren't through the arm holes, for example, but the rest of him was through the main hole, the body hole, and his legs were sticking out the bottom.

At least he wasn't running up the street in his underwear any more.

'Hey! Stop! Thief!' yelled a woman's voice behind him.

The woman whose daughter's party dress he was sort of wearing had been watching an aubergine in the front room when she saw the dress run past the window.

She'd rushed to the front door, pulled it open and shouted the words I just said she said.

Then she began chasing Fizz.

As she ran up the drive, Mr Mann ran straight into her — crash! — and they both tumbled to the ground in a big rolling heap.

Fizz didn't look behind him to see what the new noise was either. He just ran.

He ran past Mr Mann's car, turned the corner and ran towards the last corner before the park. If he could only get there before his pursuers caught up with him he'd be fine. His mum and dad would be able

to explain everything, or if not them then the Ringmaster or Dr Surprise or *someone*. He just had to keep running for another minute.

Behind him the running footsteps had started up again.

This dress flapping round his legs was slowing him. When it wasn't catching the wind like a parachute it was tangling itself round his knees like happy hour at a cub scout knot-tying weekend workshop.

He lifted the hem up, pulled the skirt of the dress above his knees and ran like that.

'Truffle!' shouted a voice, shockingly close behind him. 'Come quietly and it'll be better for you.'

'Stop, thief!' shouted a woman's voice, just as close.

Fizz darted to the right and he could see green ahead of him, at the end of this short road ...

It was the park!

And ...

His heart leapt!

He could see the blue and yellow stripes of the Big Top.

It was a hundred metres away, hardly any distance at all.

Whish!

What a strange noise, Fizz thought, as he was suddenly wrapped up like a haddock having a bad day. (I'll explain that simile in a moment, so don't panic.) He fell to the ground and rolled along the pavement. He tried getting up, but he couldn't move.

Mr Mann had seen his opportunity and had taken it.

He'd run fast, as fast as he could to beat the weird 'Stop, thief!' woman to the prize, and as they'd skidded round that last corner he'd been able to nudge in front, to get one of his leather-patched elbows in her way and she'd careened into a hedge.

Ha ha! he'd thought, like a horrible person.

And he didn't stop running, he didn't slow down.

Mr Mann had one job and he was good at it. He'd done it for six and a half years and had captured and returned to schools two hundred and seventeen and a half truants, not to mention making twice as many 'preventative pickups' (which was where, like this morning, he collected troublesome kids before they've even had a chance to bunk off). He practised at home of an evening, scouring maps, searching for hideaways, meditating. He lined dummies up in his garden and found inventive and effective means of capturing them.

He was only a few metres behind 'the girl', as close as he'd been for all the chase, and up ahead was a park. Now was his last chance. He knew when she reached the park there

 143

were a dozen different directions she could go in, there'd be crowds for her to hide in, it would get tricky.

Another metre closer and the running Mr Mann lifted his hand above his head and began swinging the 'holey cloth' that Fizz had noticed earlier. (Remember?) It was a *very* holey cloth – Fizz had almost been right. It was the most holey sort of cloth you can find. A whole bunch of holes sewn together with very fine thread and weighted with little lead balls round the edges.

It was a net.

And Mr Mann swung it like a gladiator and, at exactly the right moment, he let it fly free from his hand and with a *whish* it wrapped itself around Piltdown Truffle (as he saw things).

To you and I though, it caught Fizzlebert Stump. Like a fish. Which is what's normally caught in nets. Which is why I said what I said a couple of pages ago about Fizz being wrapped up like a haddock having a bad day. It was a most apposite simile, I think you'll agree now, even if it was puzzling at the time.

So, at the end of this, most energetic, chapter, Fizz is lying on the pavement, wrapped up in a net he can't struggle free of with a truant officer determined to return him to the school he'd only just escaped from, and all the time he can see, just ahead of him, the green greenery of the park and the bright stripes of the Big Top.

So near, as they say, but so far, as they also say.

CHAPTER NINE

In which a boy dangles in a net and
in which an old man likes potatoes

Fizz was hoisted up over Mr Mann's
shoulder and dangled, still tangled in
the net, down the truant officer's back.

The world looked upside down and wobbled from side to side as the man began the
long walk back to his car.

Fizz could only watch, helplessly, as he saw the
park and the Big Top begin to get further away.

Every time he struggled or wriggled it made the net pinch tighter around him. After a few moments he gave it up as hopeless and turned to a subtler and more classically elegant escape method.

'Help!' he shouted.

'Shut up!' Mr Mann snapped, poking Fizz with a leather-patched elbow.

'I want a word with you,' said a woman's voice from somewhere Fizz couldn't see.

Mr Mann stopped walking, shifted the net on his shoulder, and said, 'Madam, I don't have time for this. I'm duty bound to return this *thing* to its place of education. Time is ticking.'

(Fizz could imagine him tapping his watch as he said this.)

'You're not going anywhere until I get my

Josephine's frock back. And an apology from you.'

It was the woman whose daughter's dress Fizz was still half wearing.

'Out of my way!' Mr Mann barked impatiently.

'No!' she replied forcefully. 'Put the child down and give me the dress. Do it now!'

She sounded angry and Fizz couldn't stop himself from saying, 'I think you should do it.'

'You keep out of this,' Mr Mann hissed over his shoulder.

'Yeah, don't you interfere,' the woman agreed.

Then they continued their argument.

Mr Mann wouldn't give up his prize. He *would* open the net, he said, but not until they were back in school, for fear the child would

run away again. But the woman wasn't willing to wait that long to get her daughter's dress back. 'She's going to a party,' she explained aggressively.

Back and forth they traded insults and impolite suggestions, while Fizz dangled in the air behind the truant officer.

A little old man sidled into view (by which I mean, specifically, into the small bit of view Fizz could see). He was shuffling along the pavement towards the park, past the arguers, and he stopped and looked at the boy in the net.

He had a kindly face, a big bow tie and a round bald head with little tufts of hair spurting from behind each ear. In his hands he was carrying two bags of food from a popular, but cheap, supermarket.

He winked at Fizz.

'Um, could you help me?' Fizz asked.

'Oh!' said the man, seemingly surprised to hear Fizz speak. 'I thought you were a large sack of potatoes.' He leant in and peered closer, squinting his eyes and turning his head.

'But you winked at me,' Fizz said.

'I like potatoes,' the man said, twisting so he was almost upside down now, which meant he could finally see Fizz the right way up. 'They're a very sad vegetable. They often need cheering up. Sometimes a wink works wonders.'

'Could you get me down from here?' Fizz asked.

The old man lifted his hands up to show that they were full of carrier bags.

 151

'Sorry,' he said. 'I've got to get this lot home before they melt.'

'Or can you go for help?' Fizz asked, growing desperate. The argument round the front of Mr Mann was bound to end soon. This old chap was his only hope. 'Can you go to the circus and tell them I'm here. I'm going to be taken back to the school in a minute. They could come find me there.'

'The circus?' the old man asked, a twinkle in his eye. The wind ruffled his tufty hair and his bow tie fluttered. 'What does a potato want with the circus?'

'I'm not a potato,' Fizz said, hurriedly. 'I'm a boy called Fizzlebert Stump and I live at the circus. I'm trying to get back there, but I'm being kidnapped.'

'Oh no, no, no,' the man said. 'I don't

think that's the case at all. You don't look like Fizzlebert Stump at all. He's the other way up, usually, and less potatoey. And he doesn't normally wear a dress.'

'I'm not wearing a dress,' Fizz said, even though he sort of was.

'Now a *potato* in a dress, that's not so odd. I saw one at the World Circus Expo in Ipswich back in '78. It was the largest potato then known, and it was opening the fire station so it had dressed up lovely for the occasion. Had difficulty with the scissors though.'

'Hang on,' said Fizz, squinting. It was hard looking at things upside down. All the blood had run to his head and he had a bit of a headache and, on top of that, everything was *upside down*. He looked harder at the little old man. 'Are you *with* the circus?' It was unusual for

normal people in the street to know about the 1978 World Circus Expo in Ipswich.

'*With* the circus? Why, dear potato, I practically *am* the circus.' The old man stood up straight, polished an imaginary medal and then added, 'Well, I am a *part* of the circus. There's lots of us and everyone plays their part. No one is more important than anyone else.' Fizz recognised the Ringmaster's words, he was forever telling them things like this, even though some people *were* more important than others. (For example, Captain Fox-Dingle, the animal trainer, was more important than Kate, the crocodile. A circus with the Captain but no Kate would be a safe circus, albeit one with a bored animal trainer looking for a project, whereas a circus with Kate but no Captain would be a circus with

a loose crocodile wandering around with no one in charge.)

Fizz looked as hard as he could at the old man. It was difficult to tell who he was. He was in street clothes, not his circus gear. He wasn't the Ringmaster because *he* never went anywhere without his top hat. He wasn't one of the Twitchery Sisters, because neither of them were old men. He didn't look like anyone he knew.

'I'm Fizz,' he said desperately. 'I really am.'

'No, no, no,' said the old man. 'Fizz is at the circus. I saw him this morning. His parents picked him up in the woods, like you might pick a potato up in a field. If it were a potato field.'

This conversation had been so weird Fizz had almost forgotten where he was.

(However, the fact that he was dangling upside down in a net right next to two loudly arguing people, (Mr Mann and the woman had been shouting at one another all through Fizz's conversation) with the sinking sensation that he was about to be dragged back to school any moment now swirling in his stomach, did a good job reminding him.)

Suddenly the little old man flew away, zooming out of Fizz's vision.

It took Fizz a second to understand what had just happened, as the world slowly stopped wobbling. The old man hadn't flown away, but Mr Mann had just turned around, sharply.

'Who are *you*?' he snapped at Fizz's friend.

'Me?' the old man said.

'Yeah, were you talking to my prisoner?'

'Prisoner? No, no, no. I was just chatting

with your potatoes. Very impressive, I must say. Have you considered a career on the stage?'

'What?'

Fizz couldn't help but smile, even as he watched a woman walking away counting five-pound notes. (It looked like Mr Mann had ended the argument with a small cash payment.)

'The stage,' the old man said, slowly and loudly. 'Your potatoes there.'

Mr Mann grunted something unpleasant and spun around again.

He resumed walking and Fizz resumed bouncing.

'Cheerio,' called the old man, waving with a carrier bag-filled hand. 'I'll mention you to the circus. The Ringmaster will give you a call.' He made a telephone shape with his

hand, but the bag was too heavy for him to lift it to his ear. Fizz understood anyway. And what he understood was that he was never going to escape, never going to get home. Whoever this old chap was, they weren't going to send the cavalry to Fizz's rescue.

The old man turned his back and began walking towards the park, and as soon as he did Fizz knew him. He recognised the walk.

You can scrub all the make-up off a clown, you can swap their huge colourful silk costume for a shabby old suit, but you can't hide the years of training that have gone into the unique, graceful, sad, unfortunate way they walk.

Fizz had just had the first conversation he had ever had in his entire life with Bongo Bongoton, the circus's greatest (and only) mime artist clown.

And it's there, with the sinking feeling in his stomach as all his hopes drain away, that we leave Fizz. Poor boy. Captured and hauled off. Oh dear, oh dear. Whatever could happen next? You'll just have to read on and find out. Except …

CHAPTER TEN

In which we go 'meanwhile
elsewhere' and in which we go
'wind the clock back a bit, buddy'

OK, so what exactly happened last night? What have Fizz's mum and dad been up to? Have they even noticed he's missing? What did the off-duty and surprisingly talkative Bongo Bongoton mean when he said the things he said (and I don't mean the stuff about potatoes, but the bits about Fizzlebert Stump) and did he *really* mean them? (Is an off-duty clown with an unnatural interest in the potato a trustworthy source of information in this story?)

Well, let's just wind the clock back a bit, buddy, and I'll tell you just exactly what has been happening meanwhile elsewhere.

Mr and Mrs Stump heard the slam of the caravan door (we're back in the middle of the night now, keep up) and Mr Stump turned to Mrs Stump and he said, 'Did you hear that, Gloria? I reckon Fizz is back in the caravan.' And she said, 'I do believe you're right.'

And with that she pressed the button that made the clown car go and slowly they began to move off down the hill.

After five minutes the dark trees that

loomed over the road on both sides cleared and they were driving along between the first few houses of the new town where they were due to set up circus for the next four days.

'Turn left here, dear,' said Mr Stump, pointing at a road on the right.

'You mean "right", right?' said Mrs Stump, slowing the car and switching on the indicator.

'Right right?' repeated Mr Stump, getting confused.

'Right,' said Mrs Stump, turning the car.

'Where are we going now?' Mr Stump asked. 'Stop! Stop!'

She pressed on the brakes and the car and caravan juddered to a halt. They were halfway across the junction, the car nosing into the new road, the caravan parked on the old one,

but since it was the middle of the night, there was no one else around, so they weren't getting in anyone's way.

'What is it now?' Mrs Stump asked, turning to face her husband.

'You went the wrong way,' Mr Stump said.

'But you pointed over here,' his wife replied.

'No I didn't,' he said. 'All I did was say, "Turn left here, dear". Then you went right.'

'Right,' she said. 'Because you *pointed* right.'

'I wasn't pointing,' he said. 'I was doing my finger exercises.'

(As a strongman it is important that Mr Stump keeps his muscles in a state of prime physical fitness, even the finger muscles, which are amongst the most important 'picking things up' muscles there are.) (Note to pedantic people: yes, *I* know that there aren't any muscles in your fingers (they're moved by ligaments and tendons connected to muscles in the wrist and forearm), I'm not an idiot, but Mr Stump doesn't know this. No letters, please.)

'Oh, sorry,' she said. 'So it's back there?'

'Yep,' he said, pointing over his shoulder.

'Were you pointing that time?' she asked.

'Yes,' he said.

'OK,' she replied, fiddling with the gearstick and putting the car into reverse.

Before they began moving there was an almighty crash and blare of a horn and the car shuddered as a thunderstorm passed by.

'Was that you?' Mrs Stump asked.

'I don't think so,' Mr Stump replied, patting his tummy.

Mrs Stump looked into the wing mirror and saw, back to front and behind her, the whistling sight of a hurtling huge lorry. Its tail lights flashed and were gone.

They got out of the car and went to see what had happened.

The lorry blew several loud blasts on its deep parping horn as it rattled off into the distance.

The corner of the caravan that had been sticking furthest out into the middle of the road was missing. The lorry driver, who had presumably been surprised to find a caravan parked in the middle of the road, had managed to not hit it straight on, which would have made a dreadful mess, but had instead just clipped it.

There was glass in the street, and shattered

plywood, but fortunately the septic tank hadn't been ruptured so at least there was none of *that* spilling on to the tarmac.

From where Mr and Mrs Stump stood they could see into the inside of the caravan, without having to open the door.

'Fizzlebert,' his mum called, 'are you awake?'

She called quietly, because if he was still asleep she didn't want to wake him up for so small a problem.

Naturally Fizzlebert said nothing from inside the dark caravan, because he wasn't there.

'That's going to cost money to mend,' Mr Stump said, looking at the space that had twenty seconds earlier been a caravan corner. 'It's rather a nuisance.'

'I think he must still be asleep,' Mrs Stump said, tiptoeing back to the car and pulling on Mr Stump's elbow. 'Let's leave him be.'

They drove the rest of the way to the park, where everyone else was already long since parked up, without any further incident. (Except for the incidents in which they had to stop when something fell out of the caravan (a kettle, for example), and Mr Stump had to go and pick it up.

These incidents happened every hundred metres or so, and after the third time Mrs Stump said, 'Why don't you just walk along behind the caravan, dear?' And so he did and by the time they reached the park he was carrying a kettle, an ironing board, a goldfish bowl, two books on Hungarian folk customs in the seventeenth century, one book on famous fish from Swindon, a broken umbrella, a pickled stick insect, three glass eyes reputed to have belonged to Marie Antoinette, two left clogs, an empty box of instant mashed potato, three golf balls, a whisk of only sentimental value, a dumbbell, a lightbulb, a bottle of fresh Dutch wine, a stuffed stoat, a wig, a dried flower arrangement, six deflated balloons, a small chest of drawers, a goldfish, two plates (broken), one plate (unbroken), another wig, a triangular bandage, a selection of Christmas cards, a cassette tape of birdsong accidentally recorded over *The Shuffleup Sisters' Greatest Hits*, a pint of milk, a model elk, a silk glove (green), one shoebox labelled *photos (goats (funny(ish)))* and six sheets of toilet paper (unused).)

*   *   *

By the time they'd arrived and Mr Stump had unloaded himself of his load, it was very late and almost everyone at the circus was asleep. The stars were shining high overhead and the moon was hanging low on the horizon. It was a beautiful night. It was warm and welcoming.

'Let's let the boy sleep, Gloria,' said Mr Stump, sitting down beside the car.

'OK,' said Mrs Stump, opening the car door and pulling out the seats.

(The good thing about a clown car is that it comes apart easily. It's made that way. You just have to be careful not to knock the little switches and catches that hold it together when you're driving.)

'Here,' she said, handing her husband the passenger seat.

They sat down together in the soft, comfy chairs, held hands and dozed off in the open air.

They were woken a few hours later when Fish, the circus's famous sea lion, decided to check underneath them for fish. He had often found that when people were sitting down it was because they were hiding something and sometimes it turned out that 'something' was a synonym for 'fish', which just means a word that means the same thing (that's what 'synonym' means, not what 'fish' means. I assumed you already knew what 'fish' meant because you've read *Fizzlebert Stump The Boy Who Cried Fish* (and possibly even other books by other authors (I don't mind, really) that also have fish in

them, such as *The Bloomsbury Guide to Famous Fish of Swindon*)).

Mrs Stump fell off her chair and rolled across the grass.

'Arrghhh!' she shouted, climbing out of her interrupted dream.

'Oh, let me help,' said Doctor Surprise, leaning down and offering his hand. (He'd just been passing by on his usual morning stroll round the circus.)

'Thank you, Doctor,' she said, climbing to her feet and brushing herself off.

Fish, having found no fish, flolloped off. The smell, though, was hesitant about following him and hung around for a while.

'Enjoying a little al fresco snooze?' the Doctor asked, taking his moustache off and wiping it on his shirt.

'Oh,' said Mrs Stump. 'We got in later than usual and Fizz was already asleep. We didn't want to wake him.'

'How perfectly nice you are.'

'I'd best wake him now though,' she said, looking at her wristwatch. 'It's a freckle past nine o'clock. He needs his breakfast.'

'That reminds me,' Doctor Surprise said. 'Flopples needs her pre-breakfast cuddle. Must go. Cheerio.'

He dropped a little pellet at his feet and a great *woosh* of coloured smoke swirled up and around him swallowing him up. (He was, as you know, the circus's illusionist (and mind reader (and rabbit tamer)) and he knew how to make a grand exit.)

A wind trickled between the caravans and

within seconds the smoke was blown away to reveal Dr Surprise polishing his moustache on his shirt again.

'This thing keeps smudging,' he said, when he noticed Mrs Stump looking at him. 'It's new.'

And with that he wandered off.

'Morning,' Mrs Stump said to Mr Stump, who had just woken up.

'Morning,' he said back, yawning and stretching.

'Breakfast?' she asked.

'I suppose,' he said. 'What is it today?'

'I was thinking maybe toast and—'

'Post!' called Madame Plume de Matant, tottering towards them, waving a letter in her hands. 'It came to my caravan by mistake, Monsieur Stomp.' (She said it in her best

French accent, which was only slightly better than her worst French accent.)

'Thank you,' Mr Stump said, taking the letter. 'It's from my pen pal, Giovanni.'

'Ooh la la,' cooed Madame Plume de Matant. 'An Italian gent? 'ow exotic.'

'Yes, he's from Birmingham,' said Mr Stump, tearing the corner off.

'I suppose,' Mrs Stump said, 'we could have cornflakes and earthquakes, if you're getting bored of toast? I'll go get the bowls set out and you get ready to shake the caravan.'

Mr Stump was too busy opening his letter to nod, so Mrs Stump climbed up the fold-down steps and opened the caravan door anyway.

'Fizzlebert,' she whispered as she crept in. 'It's time to get up.'

Mrs Stump stood in the caravan's doorway and stared at the place Fizz slept.

The bed was folded down from the wall in the little dining area. The straps were unbuckled and dangling and the sheets were ruffled and messy. His pillow lay on the floor. But Fizz wasn't there.

'Oh,' she said to herself as she stared at the untidy bed.

Fizz wasn't there.

'That's odd,' she muttered.

Fizz was not there.

'What's that, dear?' Mr Stump called from outside.

'Nothing,' she said. 'It's just he's got up already. He's left a dreadful mess though.'

Mr Stump peered into the caravan through the missing corner.

'Oh yeah,' he said, seeing the unmade

fold-down bed. 'That's not like him. Maybe he didn't want to wake us up. You know how that thing squeaks when you fold it back up. He's a good boy, Gloria.'

'I didn't say he's not,' she said. 'But where's he got to?'

'Probably over in the Mess Tent having breakfast.'

'Of course,' she said.

She got out two bowls, lined them up on the kitchen table and poured cornflakes for her and her husband.

'OK,' she called. 'You can shake the caravan now.'

She clutched the edge of the table with her knees, and held the bowls as still as she could while Mr Stump simulated the second-best earthquake he'd ever simulated.

It was only when Mr Stump bumped into Miss Tremble, the woman who trained the beautiful white horses with feathery headdresses, an hour later, that the first inkling that something might actually be wrong bobbed to the surface of his mind.

'Mr Stump,' Miss Tremble said. 'I was expecting to see Fizzlebert this morning. Has the timetable changed?'

Miss Tremble taught Fizz entomology and astrophysics (on alternate days: insects and bugs one day, stars and space the next (she wasn't silly)), and hers were classes that Fizz actually enjoyed (he didn't understand it all, but at the very least he liked the pictures).

Miss Tremble was young and funny, she had short dark hair and jodhpurs and a sweet face and the worst singing voice you've ever

heard (although the horses liked it), but fortunately entomology and astrophysics required hardly any singing at all. She wore a bright spangly bolero jacket and a little red beret and high black boots. She smelt faintly of hay.

Mr Stump liked her, even if she did get a bit weepy when one of her horses looked at someone else instead of her. She loved those horses and that wasn't a bad quality in a horse woman.

'The timetable's up on the fridge,' Mr Stump said. 'I don't think anything's changed.'

And thus (and eventually) the mystery began.

Mr Stump went and spoke to Mrs Stump. Mrs Stump and Mr Stump then went and spoke to everyone else they could find and

soon discovered that *no one* had seen Fizz.

'Oh dear,' Mr Stump said.

Mrs Stump was more worried and said something that made Mr Stump blush and me not want to write it down.

Now, you might remember that way back in the first book I ever wrote about Fizz there was a scene similar to this one. Fizz had gone missing and the Stumps had asked around and Dr Surprise had remembered that he'd given Fizz directions to the library (and instructions to come straight back). This morning, however, Dr Surprise was of no help. He'd not told Fizz to go anywhere. But he did say, adjusting his monocle and using his best hypnotic mind reader sort of voice, 'When did you last see your son?' and that was enough to nudge the memory of the night before to the top of Mrs Stump's mind.

'The woods!' she said. 'He got out to have a pee.' (No one was embarrassed by words like 'pee' in the circus. Worse words than that could be heard when a rigger dropped a hammer on his foot or a horse forgot to tell Miss Tremble he loved her. (Sometimes, Cook even made an authentic ham and pee soup. On those days, generally, everyone chose the vegetarian option.))

'But we heard him get back in,' Mr Stump said.

'Or did we?' Mrs Stump said, ominously.

'The door slammed.'

'Many things can slam a door, Mr Stump,' said Dr Surprise. 'Why, Wilfred's Patented Sound Effect Spell makes a very convincing door slam when you shut an ordinary-looking envelope. It's most impressive.'

'Wind,' said Mrs Stump.

'Sorry,' said a passing clown (Philip T. Gibbet), 'it was those lentils.'

Within five minutes the Stumps were in the little clown car driving back up the road through the woods. (They'd unhitched the damaged caravan, so they were driving faster than the night before.)

They were, naturally, worried about their boy, left all alone in the woods all night.

'I'm worried about our boy,' Mrs Stump said.

'Naturally,' said Mr Stump, clutching his little moustache so hard with worry he left fingerprints in it. 'He's been all alone in the woods, all night.'

They zoomed along the long straight road, up the hill, retracing the drive of the night

before (but in reverse (not that the car was in reverse of course, that would be silly and Mrs Stump didn't have her clown make-up on so silliness wasn't on the cards at all)).

'Where did we stop?' Mr Stump wondered.

'It all looks the same,' Mrs Stump moaned, looking at the tall trees that loomed over from both sides.

'It could have been anywhere.'

It did all look the same, and since they'd stopped in the dark they hadn't been able to see any of the landmarks that would have helped them recognise the right place, had there actually been any landmarks for them to see, which there hadn't.

It seemed hopeless.

And then Mrs Stump said, 'I think it was just here.'

'Oh yes,' said Mr Stump, bouncing in his chair. 'I think you're right.'

What had tipped them off, what had made Mr Stump so suddenly happy and Mrs Stump so sure, was the sight at the side of the road, not twenty metres in front of them, of Fizzlebert Stump sat at the side of the road, on a tree stump, his dressing gown wrapped round his knees, looking up at the sky and biting his fingernails.

The car chugged to a halt and the Stumps leapt out.

'Fizz!' they shouted.

''Ello?' said Fizz.

'Thank goodness you're safe. You waited, you clever boy.'

Fizz nodded eagerly.

'Are you OK, son?' Mrs Stump said, spitting on an enormous handkerchief and wiping the unprotesting boy's face.

'OK? Yeah,' the boy said. 'I was beginnin' to fink you weren't coming.'

'Oh, poor boy,' Mrs Stump said, hugging her son close to her bosom. 'Of course we came.'

'Let him breathe, Gloria,' Mr Stump said. 'Give him some air.'

They bundled him into the back seat, not noticing that he was wearing a different

dressing gown to the one he'd been wearing the night before and not noticing that his pyjamas underneath weren't pyjamas Fizz had ever owned. They were too relieved to have found him more or less safe and sound to worry about little details like that.

As you've probably realised however, it's not actually Fizz they're taking home, but someone who looks enough like Fizz to be mistaken for him with a bit of mud on their face and twigs in their hair.

And so, Mr and Mrs Stump are taking the wrong child back to the circus and we'll all find out what things happen there in the next chapter.

In the meantime, why don't you have a think about how you would get on pretending

to be a circus child amongst strangers, sea lions and crocodiles. And then, if you find the thought fun and think you might be quite good at it, why not have a look in the local paper and see if there's a circus visiting your town anytime soon?

CHAPTER ELEVEN

In which the circus is returned
to and in which some things
begin to go wrong

Piltdown Truffle thought Mr and Mrs
Stump were huge idiots. What sort
of parents would mistake their own son for
someone else? Just because they had similar
not-really-what-you-can-call haircuts and
were the same height and build and she had
mud all over her face and twigs in her ears as if
she'd been lost in the forest all night ... She'd

come up with a plan to have some fun and they'd fallen for it, like idiots.

She hoped the boy, Fizz, was having fun at school. Another flipping idiot. What sort of chump puts on a school uniform when he doesn't have to! Of course it was going to get him in trouble. She'd hidden behind a tree and watched Mr Mann haul him off. She'd laughed for somewhere between five and seventeen-and-a-half minutes when that had happened.

She'd put on her scruffiest pyjamas, nicked her gran's dressing gown and struck off straight through the woods to the road the boy had been stranded on. She hadn't *exactly* known what would happen then, but whatever it was it would be better than sitting in a classroom listening to some old bloke drone on about some old rubbish.

When the stupid little car came pootling along with that pair of idiots in it she'd been delighted, if a tiny bit nervous. When the bloke climbed out he was enormous; the big muscles rippled and the tiny moustache fluttered. He was obviously the strongman the boy had said was his dad.

This was where it could all go wrong. If that monster of a muscleman thought Piltdown was trying to pull a fast one, well, she could be in a lot of trouble. But, she thought to herself, Trouble was her middle name (her parents had been astute in that) and she was certain she could bite, scratch and run faster than this man-mountain, if that's what it came to.

But obviously it didn't come to that. She was swept up in a big hug by the woman

(who looked more normal than Piltdown had expected) and had her hair ruffled by the man.

They thought she was their son. What flipping idiots!

Before she knew it she was in the back of the car being driven straight to the circus.

'Ah, Fizzlebert, there you are,' said a tall man with a shiny moustache. 'Ready for some history?'

Piltdown had been taken back to the Stumps' caravan and made to change out of her pyjamas and put on Fizz's clothes, including a stupid heavy red coat (which had once belonged to the Ringmaster, as you know). (When she'd stuck her hand in the pocket she'd found what felt (and smelt) like the remains of an old tuna sandwich.) And then the woman who was supposed to be a clown but who hadn't done *anything* funny yet fed her a second breakfast (cornflakes and cheese-cakes (Piltdown didn't complain)) and then marched her off to some other caravan and knocked on the door (it was during this time that Bongo Bongoton saw Fizz walk past the clown's caravan with Mrs Stump).

'Who are you?' Piltdown asked, trying to sound like a boy who spoke nicer than what she done talk.

'Me?' said the tall chap, rubbing his top hat. He looked surprised at the question. 'It's me, Fizz, Dr Surprise.'

'Dr Surprise,' repeated Piltdown. 'Of course.'

There were a number of reasons Piltdown

didn't like going to school. For a start she kept going to different ones. Her parents were away at boarding school (they were teachers, not very old pupils) and she had to live with her gran during term time, and, since her gran had to go where the trees were (being a lumberjack), that meant every term she got enrolled in a new school full of new kids and none of them ever much liked her.

So you might imagine being taught history by Dr Surprise, without the distraction of a bunch of other kids sitting there staring at her and whispering behind their hands, would have been a good thing, but it wasn't. Without someone to sit next to, who was there to push off their chair? Whose homework was there to scribble on? Whose pencils were there to

break the leads of? What fun was there to be had at all?

Dr Surprise sat down with the text book (*The British Board of Circus's Official Educators' Guide to the Industrial Revolution & Famous Cheeses of Swindon*) and began reading from the first page.

'Ah, yes,' he said. 'Look, Fizz. This man,' (he pointed at a picture), 'invented this thing,' (he pointed at another picture), 'which made doing something easier. See?' (He pointed at a third picture of whatever the job was that had been made easier by the thing the man had invented.)

Piltdown had never been in a magician's caravan before. She wasn't paying much attention to the book but was looking round at the decoration. There were jars and boxes

stuffed with wands and other smaller boxes and handkerchiefs and the other various paraphernalia of the illusionist's trade. Books lined the wall with titles like: *Beginners' Tricks* and *Intermediate Magic for the Intermediate Magician* and *Advanced Illusions for the Brave or Foolhardy*. From the ceiling over the sink hung a stuffed plastic crocodile from which dangled ladles and spoons and a sieve.

'Fizzlebert,' the Doctor said. 'Are you paying attention?'

'Yeah, whatever,' Piltdown said, poking her finger underneath the Doctor's rabbit. (The rabbit, Flopples, was sat on the table next to the textbook, chewing its ragged corner.)

'I'm not sure that's the attitude, Fizz,' said the Doctor, 'and please stop poking Flopples. You know she doesn't like people introducing things underneath her tummy. She's an alpha rabbit and it upsets her authority.'

'*Flopples!?*' shouted Piltdown with a sneering laugh.

She knew people gave animals stupid names, but a grown man with a rabbit called Flopples really was stupid times ten.

'Flobbles,' she said, poking the rabbit on the nose.

'Don't do that, Fizz,' the Doctor said, beginning to sound upset.

Piltdown stood up and began rummaging in a box.

'Fizzlebert,' the Doctor squeaked, standing up too, 'come out of there. Leave those things alone.'

Piltdown grabbed hold of a bit of cloth. It

had the Union Jack on it. It was like a tiny little flag. She pulled it and another flag of a country she didn't know followed it out of the box (Uganda). She pulled again and a third flag followed the first two (Vatican City). They were all tied together, corner to corner, and every time she tugged another flag flopped out.

This was fun, especially since it was making the weird old man with the plastic moustache (he'd taken it off when they'd come in the caravan and swapped it for a smaller one) upset.

'Fizzlebert Stump!' he was saying. 'Why are you doing this? Stop it! Please!'

'Sure,' she said, pulling so hard not only did three more flags (Brazil, France and Cornwall) come flying out but so did a small

bottle of smoke, which broke on the floor, smashing and surrounding them with a blue swirling fog that smelt of dolphins.

She dodged back to where the table was, and, under cover of the mist, began tying knots in the string of flags. This, she thought, was fun.

Slowly the smoke cleared (Dr Surprise had managed to find the caravan door and fall through it (which was as good a way of opening it as any, I suppose)).

'What's up, Doc?' Piltdown said, grinning broadly and swinging Dr Surprise's pocket watch from side to side. 'D'ya use this for hypnotisming?'

Dr Surprise didn't answer the question. He stared into the caravan with his mouth open,

his moustache dangling from one nostril and his monocle in the wrong eye.

'What have you done?' he squeaked, sounding like a dog toy at the end of a vigorous dog toy session when the dog squeezing the dog toy can only find enough energy for the most pathetic half-hearted little final squeeze.

The place looked a tip. Not only were books scattered around the place, not only was the broken glass of the *Dingle's Deep Sea Smoker (Second Class)* shattered dangerously across the floor, but boxes were tipped up, wands spilt out, his top hat lay crumpled on his bed and Flopples, poor Flopples, was dangling among *Flags of All Nations*, giving him the most evil look a rabbit has possibly ever given a magician in the history of the professional working relationship between magicians and rabbits, a relationship spanning over two thousand years of secret history (about which I can tell you nothing, it being secret).

Flopples twitched her nose angrily and Dr Surprise began to cry.

'Fizzlebert,' he said, quietly between sobs, 'I think you'd best go. I've taught you all I can today. I need to be alone.'

These were just the sort of words Piltdown wanted to hear. She wasn't learning nuffink about the circus cooped up in this caravan. She wanted to get out there and smell the sawdust and swing on the trapeze.

'OK,' she said, letting go of the swinging pocket watch, which flew out of her hand and through the window. (Unfortunately, the window was shut.)

She pushed past the Doctor and said, 'Don't worry, Doc. I'll let you and Flobbles alone now.' She made kissing noises and jumped down the steps.

She made her way towards the Big Top. It was obvious that was where the heart of the circus was and where all the *really interesting* things would be. They'd have trampolines and trapezes

and high wires and all that scary stuff and maybe they had lions or elephants as well. When Fizz had told Piltdown about the circus that morning, he hadn't told her everything, so there was loads for her to find out. Loads of mysteries, and her imagination helped fill in the gaps.

As she was running along, keeping her eye on the top of the Big Top, which she could see over the small tops of the caravans, she was surprised from behind and found herself suddenly screaming face down in the dirt.

'Arrgghhh!' she shouted as she writhed under the heavy dark smelly thing that was pinning her down.

It was damp and fat and unpleasant.

After the sea lion had rootled its nose into Piltdown's coat pocket and slurped and scrunched the crusty stale tuna sandwich that

Fizz had lodged there a few days earlier, it rolled off the girl.

'Urgh,' she said as she climbed to her feet, smelt the fishy waft that Fish left behind him and watched the sleek black watery beast waddle away.

'Ooh la la,' shouted a round woman with a voice like a croissant (flaky and buttery). 'Are you all right?'

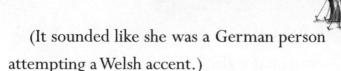

(It sounded like she was a German person attempting a Welsh accent.)

'Yeah, I'm OK,' Piltdown said. 'Just a bit squashed.'

'Is time for you to see me, *non*?'

'I dunno. Who are ya?'

'But Fizzlebert, I 'ave known you since you were a babby. Why do you say such things?'

She pulled a handkerchief out of her sleeve and blew her nose.

'Amnesia,' Piltdown said suddenly, feeling mischievous, while tapping the side of her head. 'I fell down in the woods.' (It was a good excuse, she should have thought of using it earlier.)

'Ooh la la,' said Madame Plume De Matant. 'Zat is a bad thing, *non*? You poor boy. I will make you a little thin tisane and we can go dip the madeleine, *oui*?'

Piltdown didn't know what she was talking about, but followed along because ... well, why not?

It turned out a tisane was a herbal tea and a madeleine was a little sponge cake (named after the nineteenth-century French chef Madeleine Paulmier).

Piltdown ate a whole tray of them, with Madame Plume de Matant's encouragement. After each one the French teacher (and circus fortune teller) asked, 'Do you remember anything now?' and Piltdown said, 'Nah, not really,' and Madame Plume de Matant said, 'Well, maybe just one more will do the trick.'

After all the cakes were gone and 'Fizzlebert' hadn't got any more of his memory back, she decided they'd best do the lesson anyway.

Madame Plume de Matant was relieved because the amnesia meant they could start back at the very beginning, with the French words she actually knew. (She wasn't as good at French as everyone thought, but she got by just as long as she never went to France or met any French people. (Once a French family on holiday in England had come to the show and the Ringmaster had asked Madame Plume de Matant to translate for him. After a few minutes and some not-understanding she'd had to explain to him that they spoke a rare and difficult dialect that she didn't know very well. 'But we come from Paris,' the mother of the family had explained (in English), 'how rare can it be?' Madame Plume de Matant had said, 'I must just go and powder my nose,' and went and hid in the toilet until they went away.))

'*Oui*,' she said to Piltdown. 'Say after me: "*Oui*".'

Piltdown said a different word which meant the same thing as the English word 'wee' (which sounds like the French word *oui*).

'Fizzlebert!' Madame Plume de Matant said, sounding shocked.

'Amnesia,' Piltdown said, smiling innocently and tapping her head. 'Sorry.'

The lesson went downhill from there.

Ten minutes later Madame Plume de Matant was weeping on the steps of her caravan as Piltdown ran off whistling through the circus.

This time she got to where she'd wanted to be all along: the Big Top.

Not seeing an easy way between the maze of caravans, she had climbed some crates and run across Eric Burnes (the fire-eater)'s roof. She'd then hopped across the backs of Miss Tremble's horses who were grazing on the grass on the other side, using them like stepping stones, before jumping down and, ignoring Miss Tremble's shouting and the horse's noisy neigh-saying, running the last few metres to the great striped tent.

Now, as she pushed her way through the heavy canvas tent flaps the scent of sawdust hit her in the nose. It wasn't an unfamiliar scent, her gran often smelt of it, but here in the big tent it was different. The lights were dim in the backstage area, focused as they were on the ring itself, and there was a hush in the air. After the chaos she'd caused and the people she'd upset (it wasn't her fault if they were stupid enough to get upset by her

jokes, and few things are funnier than a flying rabbit) she felt a wave of peace and calm and happiness swell up in her.

This was the Big Top. This was the ring. This was *The Circus*.

Here magic happened. Here chaos and madness and danger breathed easy, held hands and danced. She hadn't *really* known that this was what she had been looking for, but she knew it now. People showed off in that ring and everyone loved them for it. People who were different, who were unusual, who didn't fit neatly into rows and boxes, who didn't have to write essays or do sums or homework when some old bloke or some old woman told you to. The circus *wasn't school*.

Piltdown felt that she had come home. At last.

Except she wasn't home really and she knew, sooner or later, she was going to be asked to leave.

But before that happened she would have some real fun.

She stepped into the ring and began climbing the metal ladder that led to the high platform where the trapeze was waiting.

Below her, half a dozen colourfully suited and dripping-with-custard clowns were traipsing out of the ring. Obviously they'd just finished rehearsing. None of them looked up as they passed beneath. (Which was (sort of) lucky for Piltdown, since one of them was the Fumbling Gloriosus, who would've most certainly had something to say if she'd seen Fizz, or even 'Fizz', climbing the tallest ladder in the circus.)

Piltdown kept climbing hand over hand, foot over foot. After a while she stopped and looked down. She would never admit it, but she had become nervous. She was higher than she'd ever been before and until you actually get that high you don't know whether being that high is going to make you feel ill or not and, although she didn't exactly feel ill, she didn't exactly feel well either, not now she was up here.

She reached the tiny platform at the top of the ladder and hauled herself up.

The ground was so far below her it wobbled.

In front of her, tied to a pole at the front of the platform was the long bar of the trapeze.

With one eye she looked behind her at the top rungs of the ladder. They seemed so narrow and so fragile that she didn't think she'd be going down them again. The only option was to go on.

She'd swing, high above the sawdust ring. Swing and glitter and twirl in the air, like a beautiful woman in sequins. Everyone would love her for it. She'd amaze and dazzle them with her bravery and her skill. That was all she wanted. They'd pay her attention and love her.

Except she hadn't really thought this through properly (her gran said this about her a lot: 'Piltie dear,' she'd shout warmly, 'you've not thought it through properly, have you?'). There was no audience, not yet. The circus wasn't putting on a mid-morning show. The ranks of empty seats around the ring were just that: empty. But still, she was here now, and

Piltdown Truffle was not the sort of girl to turn back from an adventure.

She grabbed the bar of the trapeze and jumped into the air.

Whoosh, she went, onomatopoeically.

Her stomach plunged as she swung down and down and along and along and up and up. She yelled with pleasure into the rushing air, but couldn't hear herself for the roaring wind in her ears.

This was amazing, like being on the biggest, longest park swing in the world.

Fizzlebert's stupid coat streamed out behind her as she zoomed. Her hair ruffled. Her eyes streamed.

This was amazing.

And then the trapeze slowed, as it reached the highest part of the upswing on the far side,

and she saw a second little platform there, waiting for her to jump off. But she didn't dare: the platform looked so small and by the time she thought maybe she *would* get off, she was already plunging backwards through the air.

This was also amazing.

If only everyone could see her now. They'd forgive her for not being the best pupil there was, for being an awkward and unusual daughter. They'd simply think she was brilliant.

She didn't know it, but down below she was being watched.

The Fumbling Gloriosus had come back into the ring to look for a not-lifesize model of the Statue of Liberty she'd dropped.

She heard the yell of pleasure from above and looked up.

Imagine what she saw. (Unless we've been able to afford to get Sarah to do a drawing of it, in which case don't bother imagining it, just look at the brilliant picture. (Otherwise, imagine away, dear reader.))

There, way above her head, far up in the heights of the Big Top, her son, her little Fizz, was hurtling through the air on the rickety old trapeze, his red ex-Ringmaster's coat flapping out behind him.

'Gosh,' she said, honking her horn at the same time.

She was torn in two. Normally when she was dressed in clown gear, with her clown make-up on and her red nose resting like a huge cherry on a cake in the middle of her face, she was inclined to be silly, to make jokes and fart noises, to drop things and fall over a lot. However, seeing her son, who is afraid of heights and is rubbish at walking the high wire even when it's a low wire, swinging vertiginously above the circus ring made her want to be quite serious, because *something was wrong*.

She honked her horn and looked around for help.

'Miss Tremble,' she said, 'look!'

Miss Tremble was just leading her horses into the ring to rehearse their running around in circles act.

'Oh, Mrs Stump,' she said. 'I want to have a word with you about Fizzlebert. He trod on my horses and they're very upset with him.'

She dabbed at the corner of her eye with a handkerchief and pointed at the dirty foot-print on Emily Brontë's back.

'What? No! Look!' Mrs Stump said, pointing up.

'Is that Fizzlebert?' Miss Tremble asked. (She didn't like heights either, which is why she refused to work with very tall horses.)

'Fizz' screamed from above as the trapeze began a third pendulous swing. The two women watched.

(Piltdown had failed to step back on to the original platform and had plunged forward again. She was beginning to think this might not have been the best thought-through plan she'd ever not thought through.)

'Quickly,' Mrs Stump said, honking her horn again, 'you go get help. Find the Twitchery Sisters. I'm going to go get him.'

(Mary and Maureen Twitchery were the artistes who trapezed. If anyone could get

a rogue trapeze under control it would be them.)

'Mrs Stump,' Miss Tremble said, laying a hand on the clown's silky shoulder. 'They're not here. They've gone to Australia for the week on an exchange trip, remember? That's why Alberto McGough the Singing Echidna-Wrestler is wrestling singing echidnas.'

She pointed to the side of the ring where a large man in a leotard was wriggling underneath something that looked a bit like a hedgehog, saying, 'I submit! I give in! Help me!'

'Well, go get *someone*,' Mrs Stump said, honking urgently.

'Mrs Stump,' Miss Tremble said, quietly, pointing upwards. 'There's no safety net.'

A safety net, for anyone who doesn't know, is the big bouncy net that's strung somewhere between the ground and the trapeze so that you can fall off without injuring yourself (or worse).

Mrs Stump didn't hesitate, but began climbing.

Her big shoes didn't help.

Her wig kept fluffing against the step above and getting in her eyes.

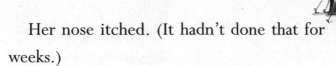

Her nose itched. (It hadn't done that for weeks.)

Her horn (which was tucked in her trousers) honked every time she lifted her leg to climb to the next rung.

She went as quickly as she could.

Step after step.

Rung after rung.

Meanwhile, William Edgebottom was sat in front of his mirror, looking himself in the eye.

He'd packed away his shopping.

He'd had a cup of tea and a digestive biscuit, and had rearranged his potatoes on the windowsill in order of beautifulness.

He sighed, looked himself in the other eye and began to put on his make-up.

Back in the Big Top young Ms Truffle was slowing down. Each swing brought her not as close to the platform as the one before had. The platforms (at either side) were getting further away.

She tried swinging her legs up, like you might do on an ordinary swing in a park, but it didn't seem to help.

And her arms were getting tired. Her hands were getting sore.

'Oh dear,' she muttered.

She didn't look down, until she did look down, and then she didn't look down again. (That didn't help much though, since what she'd seen when she'd looked down after not looking down remained imprinted in her mind's eye even when she was no longer looking down.)

Outside, Miss Tremble was running round trying to find someone to help.

'Dr Surprise!' she shouted, catching sight of the Doctor polishing his caravan.

'Miss Tremble!' he squeaked loudly, jumping with shock and turning round. 'I wasn't expecting—'

'It's Fizzlebert,' she gasped, 'he's—'

Dr Surprise waved his finger.

'Don't talk to me about that boy,' he said. 'I've had quite enough of him today. Flopples is still in tears.'

'But, he's—'

'No. Not one more word.'

And with that he climbed the steps to his front door and fumbled for his keys.

This was no good. Miss Tremble ran on.

'*Excusez-moi*, Madame Plume de Matant,'

she said in a beautiful French accent.

'What?' said Madame Plume de Matant.

'*C'est* Fizzlebert, *il est en difficulté.*'

'What?' said Madame Plume de Matant. 'Something about Fizzlebert?'

'*Oui, il est en difficulté, dans le Chapiteau.*'

'I don't want to hear another word about zat boy,' Madame Plume de Matant said in an accent somewhere between Turkish and Orcadian, turning her back on Miss Tremble. 'He's a little monster.'

And with that she walked away, leaving Miss Tremble standing trembling in the dust.

Of course Madame Plume de Matant was right, Fizz had been a little monster that morning, running over the backs of her horses when they weren't expecting it. But that didn't mean he didn't need help when he was in trouble, did it? The circus family was a family after all, and even when a member of the family acts like an idiot, you don't just turn your back on them when they need you, do you?

Not seeing anyone else about, and time being short, she ran back to the Big Top.

Over in the little caravan with the row of handsome potatoes on the windowsill William Edgebottom had vanished as if he had never existed.

In his place, in front of the mirror, with a big painted grin on his face and a bowler hat too small for his head on his head and a pair of purple silk gloves on his hands, sat Bongo Bongoton, the circus's finest and only mime artist clown.

He said nothing to his reflection, got up and began to walk over to the caravan's door.

After struggling through the invisible, but strong, wind, after pushing his way through the invisible, but long, grass and after climbing out of an invisible, but cardboard, box, he reached the door, opened it and fell down the steps into the sunshine.

In the Big Top, Mrs Stump was clinging to the platform at the top of the ladder, watching her son (as she thought) swinging back and forth in smaller and smaller swings. There was no way she could reach him. He wasn't coming close to the platform at all any more. Yet here she was. Up in the air, with a shoe almost falling off one foot, her wig askew and her nose feeling loose.

Every time she wiggled, her horn honked.

'Fizz!' she shouted. 'Just hold on! Help's on its way! Don't let go!'

Piltdown could hear the clown (the wind didn't rush in her ears any more, not now she was swinging so slowly) and thought it the most stupid load of old obvious advice she'd ever heard. 'Hold on?' Well, what else was she going to do? Let go?

She looked up at the rough canvas roof above her, and tried not to think of the ground.

Bongo Bongoton pushed his way through invisible crowds looking for his friend Unnecessary Sid, with whom he could begin rehearsing a new bit of clownish business.

Instead of Sid he bumped into Mr Stump,

who was nailing boards up over the hole in the Stumps' caravan.

'It'll have to do for now,' he said to Bongo.

Bongo Bongoton pulled a big surprised face, pointed at Mr Stump, and held an imaginary light bulb over his head.

'What is it?' asked Mr Stump.

Bongo raised his finger as if to ask for silence.

Mr Stump stared.

Bongo coughed silently and unrolled an invisible scroll.

He had news to share. Mr Stump began to concentrate. He wasn't very good at charades.

Bongo Bongoton began moving in mysterious ways.

Not far away, at that very moment, Piltdown
was dangling by one hand, thirty feet in the air.

Mrs Stump was clinging to the platform still higher, reaching out rather pointlessly with a limp fake flower that squirts water at inopportune moments, saying, 'Grab hold of this, Fizz.'

Below them Miss Tremble's twelve beautiful white horses circled hungrily, glancing up at the boy who'd trodden on them. They bared their teeth and neighed menacingly.

Piltdown Truffle was *really* worried now.

It was a long way down.

Her arm really hurt.

Her fingers were beginning to slip.

A clown was threatening her with a plastic flower that dribbled water in fat drops from the middle of its colourful petally face.

Oh, why was she doing this again?

Now the clown was honking and people were shouting.

If only she'd waited for the evening, when there would've been a crowd to see her and look up to her and applaud her and rescue her properly. But no, like a stupid person, she'd been impulsive and hasty.

Angry horses circled hungrily beneath her.

And now her fingers were really beginning to slip.

She shut her eyes as she fell.

And ...

Crikey. That was all a bit dramatic, wasn't it? It's a shame that's where the book ends, isn't it?

ONLY KIDDING

Now, read on . . .

CHAPTER TWELVE

In which discoveries are
uncovered and in which a boy
risks a mouthful of lunch

Meanwhile (actually, a few minutes earlier to be precise), several streets away and under a real roof, Fizzlebert Stump was sat at a desk, next to presumably-Charlotte, colouring in a map of the Isle of Wight, which the class was studying in order to learn the difference between blue and green. (The green went on the inside and the

blue on the outside.)

Mr Carvery was hovering over him (not in the way a fly or a kestrel or a helicopter might do, but like a teacher) tapping a ruler in his hand.

'If you ever find yourself on the Isle of Wight,' he was saying loudly in a droning-on sort of teachery voice. 'Be very careful not to stand underneath a palm tree. Up to half of all serious injuries on the Isle of Wight are caused by falling coconuts.'

In an extra chair next to the board sat Mr Mann, his feet up on Mr Carvery's desk, picking dirt out from underneath his fingernails with a penknife. He smiled to himself.

Scribble, scribble, scribble, went Fizz. He didn't know what else to do (he'd been

made to get dressed again, so he was back in Piltdown's school uniform, in case you were trying to picture the scene). He had failed. He'd got so close to the circus, but he'd been beaten, bested, caught and now he felt defeated, deflated, depressed.

But it would only be a few more hours, surely, before the school day ended and he'd be allowed to walk out of the gate and make his way back to the circus again (unless Mr Mann was planning on taking him back to Piltdown's gran). But the time passed so slowly here, sur-rounded by kids who weren't making him feel welcome (Dympna had given him a kindly sad 'sorry' smile when he was dragged back into the classroom, but she was on the other side of the room and they hadn't been able to talk again), and by grown-ups who treated him like a kid (and not a nice kid at that, but a dirty, unpleasant, vulgar one). This day would last forever and all the time his mum and dad must be going mad with worry.

That was what upset him most, the thought that they were probably still out in the woods looking for him. Unless what Bongo Bongoton had told him was right, that they'd already found Fizz and taken him back to the circus. Fizz had been hanging upside down with all the blood in his head when the un-made-up clown had said it, so he couldn't remember the exact words, but it had sounded like Bongo thought Fizz was already home. It was all so confusing.

'Keep drawing, Truffle!' Mr Carvery shouted, leaning over Fizz and banging his fist on the table.

Fizz picked up the blue pencil and began colouring the paper around the outside of the Isle of Wight.

Carefully, so he didn't go over the lines.

Meanwhile again, a mile away, back at the circus, Mr Stump had just run into the Big Top.

'Gloria!' he shouted. 'Are you in here?'

There was a distant honking high above.

He looked up.

'What are you doing up there?' he shouted, and then he fell silent.

He'd seen the colourful silky clown, way up high on the trapezeist's platform, and then he'd seen, much lower down, dangling right in the middle of the Big Top, Fizzlebert hanging by one hand from the trapeze itself.

Underneath him were a dozen dangerous-looking horses.

And between Fizz and the horses was an unbroken fall of ten metres or so.

Miss Tremble appeared beside him and said, 'Thank goodness you're here, Mr Stump. Fizz is scaring my horses.'

Mrs Stump honked her horn and pointed at 'her son'.

Mr Stump sprang into action.

He was a big man but he could move surprisingly quickly when he ran (once he'd built up momentum and especially if he was heading downhill), and he ran now, carefully pushing horses aside, and saying, 'Sorry,' and 'Excuse me,' as he did so.

In less than six seconds (but more than four) he was in the middle of the ring, lying on the ground directly underneath the just-landed wriggling shape of 'Fizzlebert Stump'.

The 'boy' had landed on Mr Stump's head, which was one of the softest landing spots in the circus.

'I'm alive!' Fizz shouted in a strange voice.

'Oh, Mr Stump,' Miss Tremble said, running over. 'You saved my horses from being squashed. You saved Fizzlebert from the fall. You are a hero!'

She helped the fake Fizz to 'his' feet, and then watched as Mr Stump clambered on to his.

There was a thin round of applause from somewhere out in the darkness.

'Very good, Mr Stump,' said the Ringmaster. 'I'm always open to new ideas, and I like this one. I have a few concerns though.'

There was a honking from above. Vigorous, urgent.

'It's not an act, Ringmaster,' Mr Stump said. 'I don't know what he was doing up there.' He turned to look at 'Fizz' who was

rubbing 'his' sore hands. 'What were you doing up there?'

'Fizz' said nothing.

Honk! Honk!

'Oh, Gloria!' Mr Stump shouted. 'Don't panic. I'll go get some custard.'

Meanwhile, back at school, Fizzlebert stood over the bin in the corner of the classroom. Mr Carvery loomed behind him and said, 'Come on, Truffle. Hurry up.'

Fizz carefully turned the blue coloured pencil in the conical hole of the pencil sharpener so that a long and continuous shred of wafer-thin wood emerged from the sharp-edged slot.

He always enjoyed this, the smell of the wood shaving, the sound of it. But he didn't

appreciate the man's shadow covering him and the impatient huffing.

'Get a move on, Truffle.'

Back in the Big Top a small pool had been filled with custard and Mrs Stump refused to dive into it, so some riggers put up the safety net.

Mrs Stump bounced happily into that.

'It's my new nose,' she explained. 'It's afraid of custard.'

Once she'd climbed out and straightened her wig, had fallen over her missing shoe and picked herself up again, Mr Stump began to tell her what Bongo Bongoton had told him.

'I just bumped into Bongo Bongoton,' he began. 'He said ... it was difficult to understand,

 244

I didn't have my reading glasses on, but *I think* he said ... "There's some fresh champagne being drunk by some dolphins and the champagne we've got has gone off." Something like that. He seemed to think it was important.'

'Champagne?' Mrs Stump asked.

'Fizz?' Mr Stump said. 'Have you got any idea what he's talking about?'

''Oo? Me?' said 'Fizz', looking pale, 'his' voice sounding a bit more like that of an unpleasant and unpopular girl than a charming circus lad.

'You OK, Fizz? You don't sound like yourself,' Mrs Stump asked.

'Fizz' kicked 'his' shoes in the sawdust, digging a little trench and not looking at either of the grown-ups. 'He' said nothing,

but mumbled under 'his' breath.

'Did someone mention champagne?' Miss Tremble said, poking her head between Mr and Mrs Stump. 'I do like a glass of fizz every now and then, just so long as T.S. Eliot doesn't know about it. He gets upset because he had some once and the bubbles went the wrong way and he sneezed in his nose bag and ever since then the others have taken the mickey.'

Mrs Stump heard a little bell ringing in the back of her mind as she listened to Miss Tremble's teary speech. (It wasn't a real bell, lodged there by an exploding alarm clock many years ago, in case you were thinking, 'Aha! I bet this is probably the cue for a joke.' It's not. The doctors had safely removed that when she was seventeen.) She took her

nose off, leaned down and looked closely at 'Fizz'.

'Freckles!' she said, suddenly.

Mr Stump stroked his moustache and looked closely too.

'Fizz' tried to turn away, tried to run off, but Mr Stump put a finger and thumb either side of 'his' head and held 'him' gently, but tightly, in place.

'Hang on, son,' he said, and began counting freckles under his breath.

He got as far as zero and had to stop, because he'd counted the lot.

'What's happened to your freckles?' he asked, quietly, not wanting to embarrass the 'boy' in front of all those horses.

'Fizzlebert' gulped and wriggled.

'I ain't sayin' nuffink,' 'he' said.

 247

Mrs Stump honked her horn and replaced her nose.

'Bongo!' she shouted.

'You mean?' Mr Stump asked, looking at her.

'Champagne,' she said excitedly, pointing at 'Fizzlebert'. 'Bubbly! Fizz!'

'I think we've got some *rotten champagne*,' Mr Stump said, repeating (the words suggested by) Bongo Bongoton's mime.

'This isn't *Fizz*,' Mrs Stump said.

With that 'Fizzlebert' kicked Mr Stump on the shin and tried to run away.

'But if this isn't Fizz,' he said, still holding on to not-Fizz's head, 'then where is he?'

'What did you say Bongo mimed?' Mrs Stump said, scratching under her wig with a rubber chicken, 'That he's been kidnapped by a group of dolphins?'

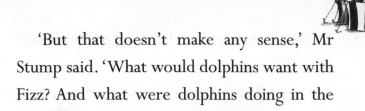

'But that doesn't make any sense,' Mr Stump said. 'What would dolphins want with Fizz? And what were dolphins doing in the woods anyway?'

'I don't know,' Mrs Stump said. 'Maybe they were foraging for acorns? Autumn's coming after all. It'll soon be time to hibernate.'

'But, Gloria ...' began Mr Stump.

While the grown-ups were talking Piltdown was thinking of ways to escape.

She'd been rumbled, found out, discovered and there was no point in her hanging around any more. It had been *sort of* fun, being in the circus for a morning, although parts of it had been too much like being at school (the bits where people tried to teach her things) to really be what you'd call 'good', other bits, like the trapezing and having cheesecake for second breakfast, had been brilliant, even the scary dangling-by-one-hand bits. If only there'd been a crowd of people to see her and to applaud her and to tell her how brave and funny and clever and brilliant and clever and brave and funny and brave she had been. And maybe give her a prize or a medal or some new binoculars. But there hadn't been a crowd and even if there had been, they'd've probably all been idiots anyway.

If only this dummy would let go of her head, she'd run off, head back to the woods, give her gran a hug and tell her what a nice day she'd had at school. But he wasn't letting go.

She'd already tried kicking him, but that had just knocked her feet out from underneath herself and left her dangling by her head until she could regain her footing. (He wasn't squeezing her skull hard, just hard enough to keep a grip on her.)

Then she noticed the big tub of custard that had been brought in for the clown to dive into (but into which she hadn't dived, being a stupid old coward and preferring the safety net). It wasn't far away at all.

By wiggling sideways Piltdown was able to get one of her feet up and over the rim of the tub and, with a bit of effort and determination, managed to tip it up, sending a glugging slow wave of yellow towards her.

'Custard spill!' shouted Mrs Stump, honking wildly, twanging her braces and

running in circles, her big shoes flapping the sawdust into the air and her bow tie spinning like a propellor.

It was a natural clown reflex.

Mr Stump, on the other hand, looked down to see his feet being slowly lapped at by the gloopy yellow mess, and immediately slipped over, *finally* letting go of Piltdown as he did so.

She sprang away, running ahead of the spreading yellow puddle, across the sawdust ring and towards the tent's exit flapway on the other side of the ring. Between her and the exit were Miss Tremble's horses, who'd huddled together for their pre-rehearsal pep talk, and fearlessly, knowing anyone who followed her would have to do the same, she ducked down and plunged between the horses' legs, and went running, running, running.

Meanwhile, it was lunchtime in the school.

Fizzlebert stood in the lunch queue, holding a tray in one hand. The other one was attached to Mr Mann's wrist by what you or I might call a pair of handcuffs (but which Mr Mann called *personal patented anti-escape child container-restrainers*). Apparently Fizz, or 'Piltdown' as he was still being called, was a 'flight risk', and Mr Mann was being paid to keep an eye on him. (Prevention, as they say, being better than chasing someone down the street shouting, 'Come here, you've got to go back to school, you rascal, you!')

He'd managed to find out that after lunch there was only an hour and a half before it was hometime. But he'd also learnt that Mr Mann *was* going to take him straight back to Piltdown's gran's house. Everything was going wrong.

What would Piltdown's gran say when Fizz was dropped off on her doorstep? Would she recognise that he wasn't her granddaughter? How would Fizz explain it to her? He could picture the scene and it was muddled, confused and complicated. He'd had experience of old women before and he didn't think back to it with fond memories. This old lady had shouted very loudly in the middle of the night, and that was when she was in a *good mood*. Imagine how she'd shout when she was given a Fizzlebert instead of a Piltdown. She might get angry. And she had an axe. Fizz stopped thinking about it.

He shuffled forward with the queue, trying to think nice thoughts, until he was in front of a pretty young woman holding a ladle.

Fizz knew all about canteens because he had his dinner in the circus's Mess Tent every night (and often he had his lunch there too, at lunchtime (and occasionally his breakfast (and sometimes, now and then, a mid-morning snack or spot of afternoon tea))). Cook dished up delightful food (ever since Dr Surprise had hypnotised him into being a Good Chef in an earlier book): big bubbling pots of stew and vats of flavourful soup or trays of sumptuous roast things. (Except on the rare and far-between days when his ears sparked and his eyes flickered and he made something like the aforementioned ham and pee soup or the not-previously-mentioned pickled egg surprise (the surprise being it was a flavour of ice cream and the second surprise being 'that's all there is!'). Mostly

Cook made the circus Mess Tent a place of
treats.)

'Chips?' the young woman said.

'Yes please,' said Fizz.

He liked chips.

She dipped her ladle down into the bowl
and scooped up five or six limp-looking pale
drooping oblongs. She dropped them on to
a plate. They went 'splat', which wasn't the
'chippest' sound Fizz had ever heard.

'Broccoli?' she asked.

Even before Fizz had said, 'Yes,' she'd
scooped a ladleful of grey-green goop up and
dolloped it on top of the 'chips'.

'Meat?' she said unspecifically, dribbling a
steaming lumpy brown slime on top of the
'vegetables'.

Fizz looked at the quivering, sloppy pile of

things he'd been given and heard his stomach get on the phone to the travel agent's to ask if there were any spaces left on the next flight to Anywhere Elseville, Farawayvia. It didn't look good.

'What do you say, Truffle?' Mr Mann hissed, jangling the handcuff.

Fizz looked up at the pretty dinner lady and said, 'Thank you,' in a small and queasy voice.

'Rice pudding?' she said, dipping her ladle in yet another pot.

'I haven't got a bowl,' Fizz said, but she wasn't listening and simply added the blobby grey paste to his plate.

'Jam?'

'No thank you,' Fizz muttered as a rocky lump of red thudded on top of his meal,

splattering his school uniform jumper with droplets of dripping 'food'.

'Yum, yum,' said Mr Mann, biting into a fresh, crisp, juicy, luscious green apple he'd pulled from his pocket.

Back in the Big Top things hadn't gone exactly to plan.

Piltdown had thought running between Miss Tremble's horses' legs while they were distracted having their pre-rehearsal team talk would have thrown any Stump-related pursuers off her scent, or at least given her a head start when it came to running for the exit, but ...

Horses have long memories, and it had been less than half an hour since this not-Fizzlebert, now darting about between their

legs, had unexpectedly run across their backs. They were still miffed. Even though Miss Tremble had given them a quick brush, and got the worst of the footprints off, they hadn't forgotten and they hadn't forgiven.

Teeth snapped around Piltdown as she dodged left and right. Big flapping flappy horse lips wrinkled and flapped and dripped horse spit either side of her as *snorfing* horse-noses nudged her this way and that.

'Now, now. Gentlemen, please,' Miss Tremble said, from somewhere near the middle of the crowd of horses. 'Leave Fizzlebert alone. He's having a strange day.'

(After finding there'd been no champagne after all, she'd wandered off to prepare her horses instead of listening to the Stumps learn that 'Fizz' wasn't Fizz after all, so she was still under the impression that 'Fizz' *was* Fizz. If she'd known 'Fizz' *wasn't* Fizz she might not have been so kind, since a member of one's (circus) family having an off day and upsetting a few people is one thing, but a stranger sneaking in and pretending to be a member of one's (circus) family and upsetting people is something else entirely.)

'No, come on, W. B. Yeats, that's not fair, don't bite the coat. Let it go. Arkle, it's not

nice to sneeze on boys. Don't do it again. No, Basil Bunting, don't trip him up …'

As much as the horses loved Miss Tremble, they didn't actually understand English (because they were horses).

Piltdown was tripped by a horse (Basil Bunting, presumably) and found herself face down in the sawdust staring at a pair of highly polished thigh-high black boots. And a little pink hand.

'Here, Fizz, let me help you up,' Miss Tremble said.

Piltdown took hold of the hand and pulled herself to her feet, but she'd had enough of this whole thing.

'Flippin' 'eck,' she shouted. ''Ow many times? I ain't your flippin' Fizzledork. I just wanna go 'ome now.'

'Oh,' said Miss Tremble, stroking T.S. Eliot's mane to soothe herself. She didn't like being shouted at.

Fizzlebert and Mr Mann sat side by side at a table all by themselves.

Fizz poked the pile of miscellaneous gloop on his plate with a fork while Mr Mann talked on his phone.

'Yes,' he was saying to whoever was on the other end, 'dreadful child. Keeps running away ... That's right, that one ... Yes, silly hair ... That's right, stupid name ... Terrible underpants.' And so on.

Fizz lifted his fork up in front of his face. The mush twitched and dripped. He put it in his mouth. (He hadn't eaten since breakfast and that burnt toast had hardly been the most

appetising meal and since then he'd run miles and suffered all sorts of difficulties. In short: he was hungry.)

He was a little surprised to find that it didn't taste as bad as it looked.

It tasted *horrible*, but it looked *revolting*.

If only lunch had been some sort of fish dish, he thought sadly. He had used fishy smells several times to attract his friend Fish the sea lion from great distances, but Fish didn't care for potatoes or broccoli or meat or rice pudding. It was hopeless.

He'd have to find his own escape route, again. But this time it would have to be better than the first time.

But what could he do? Mr Mann was going to be beside him all afternoon. They were handcuffed together now, but even in the classroom,

when they took the handcuffs off, there was no way he could make a run for it without the Truant Office jumping on him, or catching him in his net, or shooting him with the tranquilliser dart gun he'd let Fizz see was strapped to his belt.

He'd have to wait, he thought, until they were in the car again at the end of the day. You can't drive a car when handcuffed to a child, can you? Fizz would be able to open the door and then unclip his seat belt and roll out on to the road. Mr Mann wouldn't be able do anything about that if the car was moving, would he? It might give Fizz enough of a head start to make it to the circus before Mr Mann caught up with him.

But he'd have to be careful about rolling out of a moving vehicle in the mid-afternoon traffic. The rolling didn't bother him too much, he was circus-trained and was pretty good at falling and rolling without hurting himself (though it would've been easier if he'd had his ex-Ringmaster's coat to provide extra padding), but it was the dodging other cars and not getting knocked down and splatted and turned into traffic jam that worried him a little.

But he'd have to cross that bridge when he came to it.

And then he heard the oddest of sounds.

It was coming from outside.

It sounded a bit like screaming and shouting, mixed with the distant thundering rattle of a horse race.

(There'd been screaming and shouting from outside all through his lunch, of course, because all the kids who weren't having lunch at the same time as him were out there, but this was a suddenly different sort of shouting.)

And you know what shouting means, don't you?

It means I've got a headache now, so I'm going to stop writing and go have a lie down until it goes away.

Then I'll get up, have a cup of tea, and get on with writing the next and last chapter for you. Just for you. Because I care.

CHAPTER THIRTEEN

In which a rescue is mounted and
in which the circus puts on a show

Mr Mann pushed his way through the dining hall to see what the commotion was outside. Fizz had no choice but to follow, not that he minded.

When they reached the windows the truant officer carefully prised apart two slats of the venetian blinds that had been keeping the sunshine off their food and peered out.

The playground was full of horses and excited children excitedly poking the horses.

And on top of the horses were people Fizz knew.

The cavalry had arrived!

He was rescued.

At last!

He started towards the door, but when the handcuff chain reached its full extent and Mr Mann showed no sign of moving, Fizz stopped.

'Come on,' he said, breathlessly. 'That's my mum and dad out there.'

'Don't be ridiculous, Truffle,' Mr Mann snapped. 'There're too many of them to be parents. And besides, they look … strange.'

He let the blinds clatter shut and loosened the catch on his tranquilliser gun's holster.

Fizz didn't like the look of that. It wasn't friendly. But he was excited, at long last, after so long in the wrong place, he was within shouting distance of his family.

Fizz banged on the blind-covered window with the hand that wasn't chained to the truant officer. If he could attract his mum and dad's attention, then …

'Stop that,' Mr Mann shouted, pulling the boy backwards, away from the window.

The blinds rattled and popped as they unbent themselves.

'We don't know who's out there,' Mr Mann said. 'They look strange. They could be escaped from somewhere, from prison or something. I'd best call for back up.'

'They're not from prison!' Fizz shouted. 'They're from the circus! I've been trying to

tell you all along. Why won't anyone listen to me!'

He was getting angry. Once again he was so close, he could smell the smell of sawdust, and once again this unhelpful, deluded, mistaken man was stopping him. And not just stopping him, but actively ignoring him.

Mr Mann turned his back and pulled his mobile phone from his pocket. He quickly tapped three numbers in and held it up to his ear. After a moment he said, 'Yes. Get me the police.'

Outside, the rescue party milled around in the playground.

Miss Tremble had led the charge, since she was the one who could ride best.

She was sat in the middle of the playground on Basil Bunting, a handsome white horse with feathers in its headdress.

Beside her Mrs Stump clung to the neck of T.S. Eliot, another handsome white horse with an equally flamboyant feathery headdress.

Beside *her* the Ringmaster sat astride Arkle, the fastest and proudest of all the handsome white horses with feathery headdresses that Miss Tremble had ever trained. (He was the Ringmaster, so it was only right he got to ride the best horse, he said, even though he'd had to stop twice to be horsesick on the way over.)

He dabbed at the corner of his mouth with a handkerchief. He still looked a little green.

Dr Surprise and Flopples had ridden

Seamus Heaney, a handsome white horse with … Do you know what? Miss Tremble had twelve horses and they were all handsome, they were all white and they all wore showy feathery headdresses. They're circus horses, they're showbiz horses, there aren't any ugly horses in showbiz.

Eric Burnes, the fire eater, was on W.B. Yeats.

Bongo Bongoton was on Emily Brontë (backwards, trapped in an invisible box (or possibly cleaning invisible windows, or maybe building an invisible cat, it was hard to say)).

Captain Fox-Dingle had ridden Papillon. He had not brought Kate the crocodile with him, a decision he did not regret as he sat there calculating how many children it would have taken to satisfy her hunger.

Unnecessary Sid had fallen off Gerald Bostock and was honking his horn to try to keep the crowd of children that were surrounding him at bay.

Percy Late (of Percy Late and His Spinning Plate 'fame') sat astride Emily Dickinson. He looked nervous.

Emerald Sparkles (the circus's knife thrower) rode Stanley Unwin. Her sequinned top hat glittered in the sunlight and the belts of knives that criss-crossed her chest dazzled as she breathed.

Piltdown lay across the saddle of A Horse Called Sue, tied in place by some clever and hard-to-untangle rigger's knots.

And finally, on top of Sylvia Plath, sat Mr Stump, slightly queasy, sore on the bottom but eager to find his son.

'Where's Fizzlebert?' he asked a small boy who'd been busy gently poking the horse.

Before the boy had a chance to say, 'What are you talking about?', a crackling tinny voice echoed across the playground.

'Children! Move away from the horses!'

It was Mr Carvery, rolling up in his golf cart, his megaphone raised to his lips.

'And you people on the horses, go away! Clear off! Get out of here!'

Mr Stump climbed down from his horse and walked towards Mr Carvery's cart.

'Hello,' he said, holding his hand out. 'Are you in charge round here?'

Mr Carvery reversed his buggy, very nearly avoiding knocking over several children.

(The other children were mostly ignoring him and were still poking and stroking the horses.)

'Go away,' Mr Carvery repeated through his megaphone.

'Is Fizzlebert here?'

'What are you talking about?'

'It's all right, Mr Carvery, I'll handle this,' said Mrs Scrapie as she walked up. She looked the very definition of cool, calm and ever so slightly concerned as she turned to face Mr Stump. (She made sure she kept a dozen children between them as a buffer zone.) 'I'm the headmistress here. How can I help?'

Mrs Stump honked as she fell off her horse.

'Are *you* in charge?' Mr Stump asked. 'We're looking for my son. Apparently you've got him.'

'Nonsense,' she said. 'I'd remember *you* from parents' evening.' She laughed with false

 278

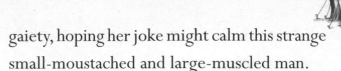

gaiety, hoping her joke might calm this strange small-moustached and large-muscled man.

Mr Stump didn't know what 'parents' evening' was and so he ignored it and just got on with what he'd come to say, 'He's called Fizzlebcrt and he came here by accident, just today.'

'No new children here today. Maybe you want St Jude's, over on the other side of town.'

Honk! Honk!

Mrs Stump wandered over, her big feet slapping the tarmac with each step. She pointed back over her shoulder with her thumb.

'Oh yes! That's right,' Mr Stump said, slapping his forehead. 'D'oh! I almost forget. We've brought you one back. To swap.'

* * *

Inside the dining room Fizz could see a bit of what was happening, but he couldn't hear any of the words.

Still, his friends were here and his heart was singing.

And then he heard the sirens.

The police were coming.

'That's my family,' he pleaded with Mr Mann. 'You've got to let me go back to them.'

'Oh shut up and sit down,' said the truant officer.

Looking around the dining hall Fizz realised they were the only people left. All the other kids had run out to see what the commotion was and to poke Miss Tremble's beautiful white horses.

No, that wasn't quite right. Dympna was still there. She was sat at a table in the corner.

(It looked like she had been sat all by herself, and not just because there was no one else there, but because hers was the only plate. The rest of the tables were covered with abandoned crockery.)

She smiled shyly and gave him a little wave.

'The circus is here,' Fizz called to her, happy and sad all at once. 'They're outside in the playground. Go and look. Go and tell them I'm here. Tell my mum and dad to come rescue me.'

Dympna said, 'I'd really like to, Fizz. Really. I want to help you get home, but I can't go outside. I'll start sneezing and crying and I haven't got a clean hanky and I won't be any good. Sorry.'

Her eyes looked a bit weepy already, just at the thought of going outside.

It wasn't her fault, Fizz knew, but it was *annoying*. He gave her a smile and, without being mean, turned back to the window.

Mr Mann was peering between the blinds again and Fizz leant forward to look too.

The truant officer was chuckling a thin little mean-spirited nasty sarcastic sneering chuckle.

Outside, two police cars had pulled up and a couple of policemen and women had climbed out and were trying to get the circus folk down from the horses and to keep the children away, and they weren't doing a very good job.

Every time they shooed the children in one direction the kids would circle back from the other, and every time they went near one horse it tiptoed backwards and the rider of a different horse would tap the police person

on the shoulder and it would all begin again. It was like trying to organise cats in a choir. That is to say, it was no good.

All Fizz needed to do was to get out there, but Mr Mann was determined not to budge.

And then Mr Mann fell to the floor in a crumpled heap.

Fizz turned around and there was Dympna holding a large can of baked beans.

'I found it in the kitchen,' she said, nodding towards the serving hatch. 'Please don't tell any-one I hit him. I don't want to get in trouble.'

'Dympna,' Fizz said. 'You're brilliant. You're a marvel. Thank you!'

Fizzlebert heaved the snoring truant officer over his shoulder and headed for the door.

'Watch out,' he said. 'Here comes the fresh air.'

He kicked the door open and headed for the playground.

He heard Dympna shut it quickly behind him and then there was a muffled sneeze, but she still shouted, 'Go Fizz!' loud enough for him to hear.

'Mum! Dad!' called Fizz, pushing his way through the crowd of children.

'Piltdown Truffle,' shouted Mrs Scrapie, catching sight of Fizz, 'stop where you are. Do not approach the weird people on horses.'

Mr Carvery drove his little golf cart directly at Fizz, but Fizz brushed it aside, knocking it over and spilling the tracksuit-clad teacher to the ground.

He said, 'Sorry,' but he didn't stop walking.

As he pushed his way through the other kids (which wasn't hard, since they saw him coming and backed away like the Red Sea had when Moses got near it in that old story), still carrying a groaning Mr Mann over his shoulder, Mrs Scrapie shouted again.

'Children, stop her! And Truffle, put that truant officer down.'

For a moment the children in the playground were torn. On the one hand, they

knew they ought to do what Mrs Scrapie told them, because she was the headmistress and the corridor outside her office had plenty of chairs for them to sit on while waiting to hear her thoughts on the depth of her disappointment at their wrongdoing and the personal pain that their disobedience causes her. But on the other (and much bigger) hand, no one wanted to get in the way of Piltdown Truffle, a girl who had been a rotten bullying nuisance ever since she first turned up the week before and who was carrying a grown (and groaning) man over her shoulder. That was a good indication of whether you ought to get in someone's way or not.

And on the third hand, there were still funny-looking people riding beautiful white horses that they could touch and poke,

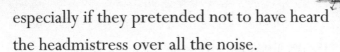

especially if they pretended not to have heard
the headmistress over all the noise.

Fizz pushed on, unhindered.

Now his dad was wading forward from the
other side.

'Fizz!' he shouted. 'There you are!'

Honk, *honk*, *honk*, went Mrs Stump as
she made her way through the sea of kids
too.

(It is hard for a clown to wade through
children. They like poking clowns even more
than touching horses. At best a horse will be
warm and furry, whereas a clown might give
you custard.)

'Mum! Dad!' shouted Fizz as he made his
way towards them.

He waved the truant officer at them.

'Young man,' said a policeman, stepping

into his way. 'Would you be so good as to put the gentleman down?'

'*Young man?*' crackled Mr Carvery scornfully through his megaphone. 'Officer, *that* is a girl and a right devil of one too.'

The policeman looked Fizz up and down and apologised. 'Nevertheless,' he went on, 'I would be most obliged if you would gently lower the sleeping gentleman to the ground.'

'I *am* a boy,' said Fizz as he gently dropped Mr Mann on the ground.

Fizz was glad to put him down as he'd started getting heavy and had started wriggling a bit too.

'Of course he's a boy,' said Mr Stump, arriving next to the policeman.

The policeman had pulled his notebook

out of his pocket and was licking the end of a little pencil.

'Name, sir?'

'Mr Stump,' said Mr Stump.

'And would you tell me why you're here in a school playground on this fine afternoon?'

As Mr Stump began to explain, and as the policeman began to write the story down (not as well or as thoroughly, it should be noted, as I've written it), Fizz knelt down and rummaged through Mr Mann's pockets, searching for the key to the handcuffs.

He'd just found it tucked inside a used handkerchief, stuck to a half-eaten boiled sweet, when Mr Mann's eyes flicked open and stared straight into his.

'Truffle,' he hissed. 'I've got you now.'

Fizz tried to jab the small key into the

tiny keyhole as Mr Mann reached down for the tranquilliser gun that was holstered on his hip.

Ting, ting, went the key as it failed to find the hole.

Pop, went the catch on the holster.

Blurp, went the sleeping potion in the gun's glass vial as Mr Mann pulled it out.

Fizz looked up. His dad was deep in conversation with the policeman.

'Dad,' he said. 'Quick.'

'Hang on a moment, Fizz,' said his dad. 'PC Gurney here is just telling me about his uncle who was a juggler with *Wally's Wondershow*—'

Fizz was on his own.

He put his foot on Mr Mann's wrist, the one that he was chained to, and heaved. The metal chain holding the two locking hoops of the handcuffs together began to stretch and screech and *POP!* just as Mr Mann fired a tranquilliser dart at him, Fizz flew fallingly and luckily backwards.

Fizz banged into the policeman and knocked him over.

Mr Stump caught his new friend before he hit the ground but Fizz fell flat on his back and watched as the feathered dart flew high up into the sky above him.

Mr Mann climbed to his feet, his face like thunder.

'You trod on my hand! You broke my *personal patented anti-escape child container-restrainers*! And they were new. You're gonna pay for that, you evil little—'

Whatever it was Mr Mann was going to call Fizzlebert we'll never know, because it

was at that point that gravity finished working its magic on the recently fired tranquilliser dart.

What goes up, the saying has it, is bound
to hit you in the back of the neck if you're not
careful.

Mr Mann fell to the floor in a slumbering heap.

Fizz got up.

'Officer,' Mr Carvery megaphoned from the other side of the pavement. 'Please arrest that girl for whatever it is she just did to the truant officer.'

PC Gurney was too busy thanking Mr Stump for having caught him to hear.

Fizz's mum finally arrived (it is always a slow journey for a clown through a play-ground, as mentioned before). She swept Fizz up into a big silky embrace at the same time as Dr Surprise brought forward a girl who looked very similar to Fizz. A girl who, in fact, looked more like Fizz than Fizz did, since Fizz was wearing a school uniform

and she was wearing Fizz's ex-Ringmaster's coat.

'What do you say, young lady?' Dr Surprise said, adjusting his moustache which had been joggled loose during all the horse riding.

Piltdown said nothing. She looked at the ground and huffed.

'Apology accepted,' said Fizz, wriggling free from his mum's cuddle. 'Can I have my coat back please?'

The crowd of kids gathered round looked at him and looked at Piltdown and looked at him and looked at Piltdown and looked at him and looked at Piltdown and then presumably-Charlotte said, 'Hang on a minute!'

When Mr Mann eventually woke up, the circus folk had all vanished and he had a headache.

 294

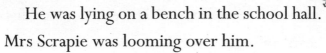

He was lying on a bench in the school hall. Mrs Scrapie was looming over him.

'A right mess you made of that,' she said. 'You brought us the wrong child. Twice. And we looked a proper laughing stock in front of the children. It's going to take an awfully long time before the little angels let us forget this. I dread to think what next parents' evening's going to be like. A nightmare, I dare say. I think next time one of our darlings goes missing I'm going to phone Stalky & Sons. I've heard good things about them.'

She took Mr Mann's business card from her pocket and ripped it up in front of him.

And then she tore up the invoice he'd left on her desk for the Piltdown Truffle job. Without paying it.

Mr Mann was not happy, but there was

 295

nothing he could do. He just hoped that news of what had happened didn't reach the Guild of Independent Travelling Truant Officers (GITTO) and get published in the 'And Now For The Funnies …' section of the newsletter.

(You'll be pleased to know: it did.)

Fizz was very happy to be back in the circus. Back with his family, his huge and extended family. The Ringmaster had him tell everybody the story of his day before dinner. Everyone laughed at him, but in a friendly way, and applauded when he first escaped the school and then cheered Bongo Bongoton when Fizz mentioned him and the conversation about the potatoes. Bongo took a proper clown's bow, fell over, climbed back to his

feet using an invisible ladder and fell over again.

Then Fish decided to take a bow, even though he hadn't really had anything to do in this book, but Cook had made a lovely seafood lasagne and there was always the possibility that a good bow might encourage someone to be generous with their leftovers.

That night the show went well. There were plenty of people in (the Ringmaster had handed out a lot of free tickets in the playground), and they did the things audiences do in all the right places (clap, laugh, cheer, go 'ooh', fall off their chairs with excitement, leave at the end of the show). Fizz was glad he'd had the chance to prove he was who he said he was in front of his former one-time

classmates. Even if he was never going to see them again it was nice to know that they knew the truth and didn't think badly of him. But all the same there was something about the show that left him feeling a bit down. He'd scanned all the faces and one had been missing.

And so, after the audience had gone, he and his parents and a few others went on a door-to-door search of houses that backed on to the park to find which one was Dympna's.

When they found it, they got her out of bed and, in her hermetically-sealed, oxygen-rich front room, put on a sawdust-free show just for her.

CHAPTER THIRTEEN
AND A HALF

**In which a loose end is discussed
and in which mutiny is mentioned**

Now, if this was a *story* and not just an accurate telling of real events, there'd be some sort of moral or lesson learnt.

For example, during Fizz's time as 'Piltdown' he would have made friends with some of the kids in the class, after having done something special and funny and wonderful for them. They would all have thought that he actually

was Piltdown and so when she was dragged back to school the next day they'd be much nicer to her and she'd be able to start afresh.

Or while Piltdown was busy being 'Fizz' at the circus she'd've learnt some important lesson about how being nice to people was better than being mean, and about how being at school and learning stuff is better than whatever the alternative is. And then when she was dragged back to school the next day, she'd turn over a new leaf, and after a rocky start, be able to become a better person all round.

Unfortunately this isn't a cleverly shaped story with a neat moral to be drawn from it. And do you know why that is? It's because I would never lie to you. I respect you, my readers, much too much to just go around making stuff up. Everything I've written is

just simply exactly what happened and sometimes real life isn't as well constructed as a
novel. I'm sorry.

So, what actually happened was this:

That afternoon Piltdown ran back to her
gran's house where she ate peanuts until her
gran came home.

She got into trouble at school the next day
and played truant again and again.

Eventually, when she turned sixteen,
without a great deal of education behind her,
she joined the Merchant Navy as a junior pot
scrubber and was involved in a mutiny off the
coast of Honduras.

The mutiny didn't go well and she was cast
adrift in a lifeboat with two other mutineers
and a small supply of biscuits and a bottle of

sparkling mineral water. (Which meant they didn't even get to play the, 'Is that still mineral water?' 'Yes, it's *still* mineral water,' game in the lifeboat, which would have passed the time quite amusingly.)

A year later she was found living wild on a desert island having eaten her companions.

Her hair had grown long and she'd trained a parrot to braid it while saying swear words.

Just before she was rescued and taken back to civilisation she was killed by a falling coconut.

If only she had tried harder to be nice to people at school and had paid more attention in class.

So, maybe there is a moral to the story after all: *Children, beware coconuts.*

HAVE YOU READ FIZZLEBERT'S FIRST ADVENTURE?

Fizzlebert Stump lives in a travelling circus. He hangs
around with acrobats, plays the fool with clowns,
and puts his head in a lion's mouth every night.
But it can be a bit lonely being the only kid in the circus.
So one day, Fizz decides to join a library – and
that's when it all goes terribly wrong ...

The bearded Barboozul family are the new stars of
Fizzlebert Stump's circus. Their act is full of magic,
mystery, fun and fear. But then things start to go wrong.
The lion loses his dentures. The clowns lose their noses.
The Ringmaster loses his temper. And the circus is about to
lose its licence. Is the bearded boy to blame?

HAVE YOU READ FIZZLEBERT'S THIRD ADVENTURE?

When Fish the sea lion goes missing, Fizzlebert tracks down the runaway beast to the Aquarium, with its piratical owner Admiral Spratt-Haddock. But the Aquarium has problems of its own. Fish (not Fish the sea lion, *fish*. Keep up) are going missing, and the Admiral blames the circus. Can Fizzlebert solve the mystery?

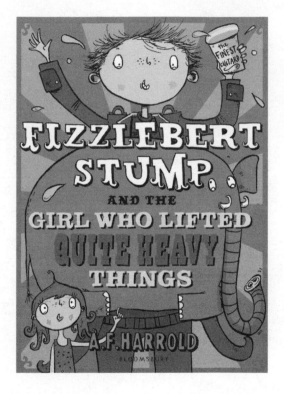

It's the great Circus of Circuses competition, and Fizzlebert Stump has no act. He's no longer the Boy Who Puts His Head In The Lion's Mouth – the lion retired.

Can Fizz find a new act in time? Can the Bearded Boy find his long-lost parents? And can their new friend Alice, secret Strongwoman, find her rightful place in the circus?